ICE MAIDEN MELTS

ICE MAIDEN MELTS

LARISSA LOVEJOY

Perspicuous Press

Contents

1	1
2	11
3	23
4	34
5	43
6	51
7	61
8	70
9	78
10	85
11	92
12	100
13	108
14	117
15	125
16	132

17   140

18   147

19   154

First Printing, 2022

Cover Credit: alexandr_1958

ISBN 978-0-6451422-6-6 (pb)
ISBN 978-0-6451422-7-3 (eb)

I

Marcia Knight was every bit as sassy as her name sounded. She looked intently at her reflection in the mirror. She applied no make-up except for her trademark, glossy, red lipstick. Not displeased with her image, she stepped back, and smoothed her hands over her shapely hips, enjoying the fresh touch of her linen suit. It was new, plain navy, and understated, very suitable for her first day of a new job.

"Mm, Dr Marcia Knight," she said out aloud, "you'll pass the test, I think. I sure hope so."

Marcia pulled her hair back and twisted it into a chignon. The blonde hair immediately unravelled. It was in that awkward in-between stage of being almost shoulder-length. The novelty of having it cropped short for the heat and informality of the conditions of her previous job had worn off, and she welcomed the familiar return of length, body, and curl. In this new job, she'd need to tie it back, but today it didn't matter. One last brush was all that was required, and she was ready to go.

While it was early morning, the Australian heat was already evident, and she was glad of the air conditioner in her new, sleek, red Jaguar, a coming home present from Daddy. Part of her wished he didn't spoil her in such ostentatious and extravagant ways, the other part of her, the bigger part of her, relished his generous attention. Why shouldn't she? There was no other man in her life.

The distance from her new apartment in a leafy suburb, to her new place of appointment, was short, and she winced a little with slight embarrassment as she noted the older cars parked in the staff car park. Her car stood out. Perhaps she might walk to work in future, as she had done in her previous job in the far north of Australia. But it was stifling hot, and she hated feeling sweaty.

She parked her car beside a dilapidated, white Volkswagen with "save the health system," and "children matter," stickers randomly plastered over the sides and the front bonnet. Something about the car looked familiar. The owner uncoiled his enormous frame out of the tiny beetle car, and called out, "staff only, my dear."

Immediately despising this man's patronising tone, Marcia retorted, "I am staff," then aware how standoffish she must have sounded, added shyly, "new staff."

Marcia was intent on getting into the hospital building as quickly as she could, the air was already a trifle sticky, and the humidity would bring out her curls. This man's dominating presence was unnerving her. Not that she was looking at him, or taking him in, but out of the corner of her eyes, she instantly noted he was everything she loved in a man; he was tall, broad shouldered, and exuded a commanding sense of presence. Her eyes dropped as she saw him move toward her and stand blocking the staff entrance.

A deep, friendly, masculine voice asked, "so you must be the new Dr Knight then?"

There was something about his voice that jolted her. "That's right," replied Marcia, only now looking up to meet this man's eyes. Her bright blue eyes met his deep dark brown eyes, and they stood transfixed, neither able to speak.

After a short time of silence, the man took a deep breath. "Marcia?" he asked tentatively, but not needing an answer.

"Joel?" she asked in disbelief, shock, and she had to admit, slight horror.

"Oh Marcia, I can't believe this," and seeing her face pale with surprise, he grasped her arm, and pulled her gently into the entrance, ushering her into a small, side waiting room.

The touch on her arm made her shiver with its familiarity, and as he moved closer, to embrace as old friends might, she grasped his arm coldly, and thrust him away. There was no way she was going to let him know how her heart was racing at pace, a crazy pace.

"Joel," she hesitated, "Dr Trucker, I guess I should call you here, why didn't you know it was me coming here today? Why didn't you alert me to the fact that you're here at this hospital? Why didn't you tell my father? Why didn't he tell me? Why aren't you still in Melbourne?"

Instead of being disgruntled with the barrage of questions, Joel guffawed, a loud, hearty, warm laugh that Marcia recalled so well that she resisted an instant natural smiling response, one most people would find it impossible not to give. He knew her reactions and understood how to read the impatience on her face for his answers. He tried to calm her by placing his large, tanned hand on hers, but she thrust it hastily aside.

Still smiling, he said quickly, "like you, I escaped and went away, and like you, I came home again, but much quicker than you did."

"I don't think it's as simple as that." Marcia's face glared with an animosity she felt confused with. Why, oh why, was her first day on this job going to be ruined by this handsome man who she had spent so many years trying to forget?

Whatever Joel read in her face wasn't troubling him at all. "You forget my lovely one, that I..." but whatever he was about to say was interrupted, the sentence was left unfinished, dangling in mid-air.

This time, Marcia grabbed his hand, squeezing it somewhat menacingly, and said, "presume nothing, Dr Joel Trucker."

"I won't, Dr Marcia Collins."

"Joel Trucker, if you ever call me that again, I'll, I'll...." And this time she couldn't finish the sentence.

Joel was standing so close to her that their bodies were parallel but not touching. She could feel his energy radiating around her. Sometimes, she thought that was merely hippie talk, but no, today, she felt the energy, like an aura. Their bodies were heaving rhythmically, in tune with their high-intensity emotions. Disturbing passion was unwelcomed on this important first day of work, but its presence overwhelmed Marcia, she couldn't deny it, and she wanted to fall onto that impressive chest that lay dangerously close to her.

"Come on Marcia," Joel said quietly, "understand my position. I wasn't on the selection committee for your appointment, so I didn't see your curriculum vitae. I was away, giving a conference paper in Sweden. All I knew was that the new doctor had a lot of experience in the north of Australia, working particularly with Aboriginal children. At first, I thought it might have been you, but I didn't recognise the name Knight. If I suspected that the number one candidate, was you, I would have looked for a Dr Collins, isn't that right?" His look turned to bewilderment as Marcia's face was blank, but gently probing, he asked, "and who is Dr Knight?"

"Me, Joel," Marcia said, blue eyes blazing in fury, "and don't you ever forget it."

"Why Knight?"

"It was my mother's maiden name. I wanted a new identity when I went north, so I took on her name. It helps me to feel closer to her."

"You were escaping, just like me." He paused, his probing eyes locked onto hers. "How did you get around the legalities of your medical certificates being in a different name?"

"I explained the bare minimal of my situation. They understood. They were desperate to employ me."

They stood facing each other, years of memories brimming to the surface, emotions bubbling in a hot cauldron.

Marcia noted that Joel's appearance hadn't changed much in the five years since she'd seen him last. But there was a novel attractive look of maturity she had not seen before. He stood a full head taller than her height, and she was tall for a woman. His broad shoulders were visibly heaving up and down as he breathed deeply, clearly affected by this chance meeting. Is anything chance?

He wore crisp navy trousers, a white shirt, and a comical Mickey Mouse tie that the sick children they attended to, would love. His skin was clear and fresh, a man who spent as much time outdoors as he could. He was highly tanned, she knew of his love for the ocean. He hadn't lost his boyish habit of pushing his hands through a mop of unruly, dark, curly hair, that had a reddish glint when he was out-side or under the light. His dark eyes signalled a swirl of meaning; she could sink into the pool at any time if she didn't watch herself. Without a swimming costume, Marcia felt herself being pulled into the depths, dragged deep, and instinctively couldn't take her eyes away. She was light-headed, almost drowning.

Desperately wanting to submit, afraid that he was going to pull her to him and wrap his long, secure arms around her, and never let her go, Marcia stepped back as she heard a woman's voice outside the room, and a nurse blustered in.

The woman who burst in was a picture of beauty. She had long, red hair tied haphazardly back, although the loose, wild, ringlet curls were desperately, and successfully, trying to escape. She had a wonderful sense of liveliness about her, and with a lilting Irish brogue, she almost sang, "oh Joel, I thought I saw you," and she laughed in a free, relaxed manner, as Joel placed his hands on her bottom, brought her to him, and kissed her full on the lips.

Marcia turned away, astonished, embarrassed, and angry at herself for feeling uncontrollably jealous. This was no proper start to her new job. Work was her life. It kept her sane.

Nothing seemed to worry Joel. He whispered to this nurse for a while, and then pivoted her around so the two women were facing. "Dr Knight, meet nurse Una Byrne, our resident Irish Colleen, the apple of many a man's eyes." The woman laughed easily, Marcia didn't, but she took the hand offered and shook it, not reciprocating the friendly smile.

"We are a very close team here at the Children's Hospital," the nurse said, giggling with Joel. "I'm very pleased to meet you. I hope you'll be very happy here."

Marcia looked at her watch and grimaced, she hated being late. Una noticed her anxiety and reassured her. "We're in good time. I've come to collect you both, to take you to the Director," and she marched off in haste. The Director was clearly not someone to be kept waiting.

Joel walked beside Marcia, close, but not quite touching. "How close a team is this, Dr Trucker?" asked Marcia, still surprised at Joel and Una's intimate greetings. Her face was grim. Icy cold. She shivered with nervous anticipation.

"Oh, very close, Dr Knight." His grin was wicked, decidedly mischievous.

"You always were very forward, Joel."

"You have become strangely prim, Marcia. In fact, you appear as an Ice Maiden." Marcia looked straight ahead.

Hospital corridors are long, and Una marched off at a cracking pace, almost intuitively knowing when to slow down for Joel. Marcia couldn't be anything but impressed with Joel's obvious popularity. Everyone appeared to know him, some calling him "Joel", others more formally, "Dr Trucker". He had a kind or witty comment for all and sundry, and he seemed to know the names of the porters, the nurse assistants, the senior nurses, secretaries, cleaners, and consultants. Marcia was vividly aware of his presence beside her. It was impossible not to. Her heart was pounding.

Eventually, they arrived at their destination, and Marcia was surprised to see a small room full of twelve people. She recognised a few faces from her interview. The Director explained that she liked each working unit to meet at the start of the week, and this was a good time to introduce the team to Dr Knight, the new anaesthetist to the general surgery section of the Sydney Children's Hospital.

Marcia felt unusually startled when the Director asked her to tell the group a little about herself. It was a perfectly reasonable request. Normally, she was an easy, confident public speaker. She often gave talks about health to school children, and she loved speaking at mother and toddler groups. Today, the presence of the tall, handsome man whose eyes never stopped dancing in her direction, annoyingly unnerved her.

Their eyes met across the room. For a few seconds, it was as if no one else was in the hospital seminar room except themselves.

"I can introduce Dr Knight," Joel said unexpectedly, an authoritative look of triumph on his fine-looking face.

"Oh, do you two know each other?" the Director asked, clearly surprised.

"Not in the Biblical sense I hope," quipped Una gleefully, as everyone bar Marcia laughed easily.

Quick as a flash, not giving Joel the chance for any further exposure, fearing what he might say, Marcia retorted, "we know each other from the past, we were at university together."

"Why didn't you mention that Joel when we were going through names?" the Director asked.

Please God, cried Marcia to the heavens, please don't let Joel blow my story. I might have graduated as Dr Collins, but I am now Dr Knight for very good reasons that no one here needs to know about. She sensed bemused faces looking at her and Joel. She avoided his gaze, embarrassingly conscious of those dark eyes penetrating through to her innermost being. They kept reaching their target, and she shivered inside.

After what felt like a long time, but was only a few seconds, Joel responded in a voice less animated than usual. "Medical school seems a long way back. I've been in Melbourne, Dr Knight's been up north. We're both back in Sydney with wards full of sick children, and we all have important jobs to do."

No one seemed entirely convinced by the reply, but Joel's charm carried him through. As usual.

Marcia took a deep breath and introduced herself briefly. In an offhand manner, she signalled toward Joel, while avoiding eye contact. "Yes, I was at Melbourne University with Joel, we both were awarded scholarships. I specialised in anaesthesia. Apart from some holiday travel, I'd never seen much of the north of Australia, so I went to the Northern Territory to work with Aboriginal children. It was a fascinating time. I learnt an incredible number of new ideas about general practice, as well as my specialism. However, it's very hot, and the presence of scary crocodiles means you can't swim in the rivers or ocean," and she paused while the group laughed. "Besides, my father is getting older and lonelier, and I wanted to return home to spend more time with him. I was delighted when this vacancy arose, and I'm very pleased to meet you all."

She meant this. The group members were friendly, open, and warmly welcoming. All of this augured well for her future career, except for the dominating presence of one man, Dr Joel Trucker, sitting the other side of the table. How could he affect her emotions so quickly?

She watched as he thrust his hand almost boyishly through his curls, hair which instantly flopped back into an unruly, but attractive state. The gesture was frighteningly familiar. The action was sensual, and she almost felt aroused by watching it. This would not do. She was a highly trained medical professional. These feelings were inappropriate responses to another colleague. That's all he was to her. Surely, that was true. She had to kept reminding herself of this. As the chief surgeon, she supposed he was her senior. The group appeared to be very unconcerned with status and rank, preferring an egalitarian approach.

The Director thanked Marcia for her introduction. She carried on in her customary bustling manner. "We work as a very close team," she began, and Marcia caught the cheeky grin between Una Byrne the gorgeous Irish nurse, and Joel Trucker, the overwhelmingly handsome, paediatric general surgeon.

Were they a couple? They had to be. Surely. But why didn't they arrive together in the same car? Did they embrace every morning at work, and so public at that? Did Joel kiss her daily on her luscious lips in front of everyone? Did they fall into each other's arms at the end of the day, and wrap their naked, yielding bodies around each other? Marcia was startled at the way her mind was wandering away. This was absurd. She was at work.

Marcia realised that day one on a new job is crucially important. The Director was droning on, summarising the last week's work, giving out instructions for this week, clarifying answers to questions staff were asking.

Marcia's mind shot back with a whirl as the Director called her smartly to attention. "Now Dr Knight, as I said, we work as a friendly team here. We're on first name terms if there are no patients around, or when they are nicely under your anaesthesia. As a good practice, we use this team of twelve as much as it is possible to stay on the same shifts. Each month, we change the nature of the group a little, to keep a dynamism alive, but a month is a good time to build a sense of team effort. This is the team for this month."

"That's admirable," Marcia responded, gritting her teeth in

realisation that she'd be working in such proximity to Joel. She had no idea how she would cope, working in his presence. Her professional voice took over. "I'm also a firm believer in a good team spirit in the wards, the children respond favourably to it."

"Yes," the Director barked in the matronly way she had of appearing gruff, but simultaneously, everyone knew how infinitely kind she was. "We operate the same principles for surgery. This month, you'll work with Una as the chief theatre nurse, and you will be the anaesthetist for surgeon Joel."

Marcia looked at pace from the Director to the gorgeous nurse with bright red curls, to the stunning man sitting opposite her. She couldn't fail to see the elation written over the faces of both nurse and doctor. She sat, trying desperately to maintain a professional persona, but feeling she was failing. Her heart was beating too quickly.

She took a deliberate, slow breath, and then another. She had done courses in yoga and meditation. It would be alright, it had to be. Would it be?

2

As she sat in the same room as Joel, a million memories flashed through Marcia's brain, some welcome, most unwished-for. How dare Dr Joel Trucker walk back into her life again? How dare he disrupt her chance of settling back easily into Sydney, and what was her home city, as well as his.

She wondered if her father knew about Joel's presence in the hospital, they used to be extremely close. Quickly, she realised that he would certainly know that Joel was a surgeon at the hospital, perhaps he had chosen not to say anything to either of them, for motives only he appreciated. The realisation that she hadn't even asked her father where Joel was based annoyed her. That was ridiculous. Yes, she concluded, naturally her father would know exact details about Joel's whereabouts and life. For his own reasons, he must have decided to keep them from his daughter. She would ask him as soon as she could.

Five years was a long time to be away, and she had been so busy settling into her new apartment, that she hadn't had time to meet up with old friends or catch up on the local gossip. Once upon a time, almost all her friends were Joel's friends also. What did this mean now? Was she destined to bump into him socially, as well as at work? That couldn't happen. She'd make sure it didn't occur.

Why, oh why, had nobody told her that Joel had returned from Melbourne? But of course, he would have wanted to return, to come home. She should have known this. She felt very flustered.

Then she shifted irritably in her seat. Why should this man bother her at all? She was a highly capable doctor, she knew that, and everyone she had ever worked with reassured her of this fact. Her references were outstanding, she had felt extremely proud reading them. She loved her work, kept up with current reading in her field, knew all the latest medical trends, and was careful, concerned, and interested in every one of her patients. Her job demanded this attention. Every precious life mattered, and she made sure that her patients grasped how important she considered their welfare.

Caring for sick children in the hospital had taken central place in her life during these past years. No one else had figured as significant, except for her father, dear old Daddy who spoiled her rotten since her mother tragically died in a car accident, two years before she graduated. She had coped with her mother's death by throwing herself vigorously into her medical studies, appreciating that this is what Mummy would have wanted. In the absence of a son, her mother had dearly wished for her daughter to follow in her darling husband's footsteps into medicine. She had fulfilled her mother's wishes admirably.

Then, there had been a time when Marcia had to decide whether to specialise, and if so, in what direction. She resisted yielding to her father's non-too subtle pressure to follow him wholeheartedly into surgery. He had been delighted when Joel had chosen this direction. Her father had pushed Joel's destiny toward this objective. For reasons Marcia was never quite sure of, it was anaesthesia that was her prime interest, and she followed her heart, as she was prone to do, back then. Her career was the only area of life where her heart's yearnings were kind to her.

Men certainly had figured in this past period of her life, men who'd caused such intensity of pain, such a brokenness of spirit, that she could only cope by fleeing as far away as possible. Her first hospital appointment in the north of Australia was a lifesaver. It had given her a chance to resurface from the troubled waters she had found herself splashing in. It stopped her from drowning. Nothing else mattered to her except establishing her career, and helping sick children breathe comfortably and safely during surgery.

Marcia's thoughts of the past were startled back to reality by a deep masculine voice repeating the words, "you, Una, and I, will make a fine team."

The permutations rolled over in Marcia's brain, you and me, Una and me, you and Una, me and you. What was happening to her emotions? They had gone helter-skelter, turbulently crashing in a rollercoaster of frenzy. She hated fairgrounds. Her professional front permitted her to stammer, "great, that sounds fine."

"Right then Marcia, Andy and Shona can show you around," and Joel put his arm protectively around the shoulders of the two youngest nurses in the room. They beamed up at him in conspicuous admiration.

Did everyone adore this man? Marcia wondered, then countered this by reminding herself that if there was anyone who didn't adore this man, it was her. She had every reason in the world to despise this man, or so she kept telling herself. Was it true? Could it possibly be the case? If it was, why was her heart fluttering away?

"Please be back in one hour, we'll be ready to scrub up for surgery, Marcia," clarified the lilting Irish voice of nurse Una.

"Surgery this morning?" queried Marcia, looking at Joel and the Director, "but I like to talk to the children before surgery, working out exactly what I'll require for anaesthesia."

"There's no time to do that this morning Marcia, I respect your position and I am sorry," replied the Director. "I have had the consultants do the rounds last night, you will be able to check their detailed notes. There will be time later this afternoon to do your ward round and meet tomorrow's batch of patients, and start afresh."

Simultaneously, everyone saw that the briefing was over, and stood to scamper off to their respective tasks. Marcia hovered back, letting others leave ahead of her. She felt the familiar presence of Joel behind her. She didn't turn around. He blew gently on her neck, and she shivered gloriously. She knew that he was bending down slowly to her ear as she felt his warm breath on her neck, and he whispered in her ear, "my God Marcia, you are even more beautiful than I'd remembered."

For a moment, she was sorely tempted to lean back on his comforting chest, but she resisted, and stormed off in fast pursuit of Andy and Shona, without a look behind her.

These nurses were lovely young people, and she was grateful for their good-natured humour, spontaneity, and laughter, as they took her on a whirlwind tour of the hospital. They too seemed to know a lot of people and stopped to speak briefly to those children they had already met, or who seemed to need a quick word of encouragement. Here, Marcia was in her element. To witness children break out into a smile, gave her all the pleasure she had needed over these long, lonely years. She had known no other desire than the yearning to help sick children become better, and sometimes, to help save the life of a dying child.

The hospital had a lovely atmosphere. Brightly coloured posters and paintings were hung at child height on the walls. Animal mobiles dropped from the lights. The curtains were brightly coloured. Murals adorned the walls. Nursing staff wore traditional uniforms, in pleasant colours. Medical staff wore coloured coats instead of the usual, austere, clinical hospital white. Name badges had a picture of an animal. Marcia was amused to see that her badge was a big, black cat. She had never liked cats. She wasn't an animal person at all. She'd never had a pet as a child.

Too quickly, Andy and Shona brought her back to the small rooms beside the surgical theatres where staff met for last-minute discussions. Una gave her a brief, but very thorough and impressive overview of the morning's surgery, and left her to study the suggestions given by the consultant anaesthetist. Satisfied, Marcia went to gown and scrub up, knowing that Joel would come in a little while after her, while she was preparing the first patient.

While she changed into theatre gown, slippers, and cap, and stood methodically scrubbing with antiseptic lotions, she had time to think about the fact that a child's life was about to be in her hands. She had never lost the wonder of the task ahead of her. More than once in an emergency, she had called out to God to help her, and since then, she always kept this time of preparation to prepare herself mentally for the enormity of the duty ahead of her. This was her calling.

Today, her usual reverie was distracted. How would she feel working on such a crucial job with this man whom she had fled from? All these past years, she had tried to persuade herself that she despised Joel, resented him, loathed him, even hated him. Hated him? Did she really? Could anyone hate Joel? Surely, it was not possible. Did she have any good reason to do so?

Marcia thought that she had rationalised everything there was to excuse about her past, including Joel's role in it. Of course, she had to flee for all these years, partially to escape from him. But, seeing him in the flesh again presented a different scenario. It was like being in the presence of someone who made you come alive. She saw him swish past the window and wink at her. Damn him, how dare he undermine her professional status like that! She wasn't someone to be winked at.

She moved into the pre-surgery room to talk briefly to the young patient. In a soft reassuring voice, she talked quietly to the little girl, stroking her face gently, reassuring her mother, and asked the child to count to ten. The simple trick always worked. With a quick un-obtrusive jab of the anaesthesia, the girl only had a chance to count to three, and she was away with the fairies. Her mother smiled and went reassured to the parent's waiting room. Marcia didn't approve of parents staying this long. In due course, she vowed to let the Director know this, and ask for a change in policy.

Marcia's first thought on entering the surgical theatre, was, why oh why, is this first operation for a removal of the tonsils? This meant that Joel would be standing right up beside where she worked, monitoring the breathing, heart rate, and pulse. Why couldn't the operation be for the toe, far away from her?

She had nothing to fear. Joel was a wonderfully confident sur-geon. He made his team feel comfortable and secure. He let them know how serious the occasion was but let them smile in-between urgent actions. He was thoroughly in command, yet totally sensi-tive and flexible to the staffs' needs. He encouraged and praised them constantly. They responded in devotion to his every look and request. Obviously, this was a highly respected doctor in full com-mand of his surgical theatre.

Several times, Joel moved to get the perfect position to operate, and his body brushed against Marcia's. Suddenly, she felt virginal, as if no man's trouser legs had ever brushed against hers before. She had conducted thousands of anaesthetic procedures, yet in the presence of Dr Trucker, she felt a novice, not unprofessional, just not as confidently, self-assured as she typically felt.

Joel continued to encourage the whole team, constantly re-assuring them, encouraging everyone with words and eye contact, making each staff member feel like an important part of the team. He was a very smooth operator, no wonder everyone loved him.

After each operation, they stopped for a quick drink of water, a brief break, then scrubbed up again, ready for the next patient. Even a late lunch was slotted in a passing fashion. It was a hectic schedule. At least Marcia didn't have to work at the furious pace that Joel did. Certainly, she kept a constant monitoring of breathing patterns, heartbeat, and pulse rate, but she could do some of this sitting down. That gave her the chance to observe activities.

Joel and Una worked as one. He rarely had to request a specific surgical instrument, Una intuited precisely what he needed, and when he needed it. As senior theatre nurse, she kept her team on their toes, keeping the theatre processes flowing smoothly. She too was encouraging to those nurses she was mentoring. Joel's concentration never left the patient, yet Marcia felt that he saw that her eyes were often on his. Magnets inescapably drawn together.

She was glad when the day's surgery was over. At last, she could do a hospital tour by herself, visiting patients who would be operated on tomorrow, without the intensity of the team hovering around her. She admired the principle of close teamwork, but it meant that there was never a moment to oneself. Someone in the unit was always there.

Marcia's time away from all that was well-known had taught her the value of solitude. She often went hiking with a carefully packed backpack, alone. She spent most nights at home, alone. Solitude allowed her to gather her thoughts, and she needed space by herself to do this. Joel's constant presence was unnerving.

At the end of surgery, she finally thought she was alone, and flung her surgical gown off. She heard a click as if the door was being locked. It was.

"Joel, open the door, get out, don't be ridiculous, leave me alone," she screeched in a high tone, not wanting to raise her voice, and be heard.

Ignoring her, the direct comment came, "mm, very nice indeed."

Joel's eyes unashamedly focused on Marcia's cleavage, her top was far more exposed than she had realised.

Marcia went to grab her green surgical gown, but Joel beat her to it, and deftly threw it into the laundry basket along with his. He stood there in his loose, white, cotton surgical trousers and top. She sat in her loose, white, surgical dress with the deep vee that was generally covered by the overlaying, unglamorous, green surgical theatre gown she wore over this dress.

Trying to be unaffected by his presence, she coolly said, "would you mind leaving? I need to shower before doing my hospital rounds."

Joel laughed as he frequently did and came across to her. He took her cold hands in his warm ones, and tried to get her to stand, but she resisted. "Where have you been, my lovely one? Any medical staff on this floor who want to shower after surgery, come here. We have our clothes lockers in this room. These change rooms are entirely unisex, welcome to the twenty-first century darling, where have you been?"

Marcia looked frightened. "I couldn't change here in front of you."

"Why not my beauty? I've locked the door, you could do more than change in front of me. Do you think I haven't seen your beautiful body before?" He let this sink in, as both recalled countless times in the past when they had undressed openly together, usually to go swimming.

After a while, Joel turned away, casually informing her, "you can change in the shower cubicle and shut the door, there is privacy if you need it." No words came. Unusually, Marcia was flummoxed. She glared at Joel with such a cool intensity that he just laughed. "Go on Marcia, have your shower, there are locks on the cubicle door to keep the likes of me away."

"Away from the likes of the adorable Una, you mean?"

"She is lovely, isn't she?" Joel grinned in seemingly lustful admiration. But then, you couldn't be totally sure, he grinned at everything. "Nursing staff and medical staff don't shower together."

"At hospital you mean?"

"You're a quick learner, you always were." Was he mocking her? Probably.

The light-hearted banter stopped as the sound of water from two showers started to flow. Marcia noted through the slats on her door that Joel didn't bother locking his door. The silence was powerful. Marcia could imagine Joel's body, tall, broad shouldered, taut. She wondered what he would feel like, wet, slinky, smooth, hard under her touch, then again, she kicked herself for falling so quickly for his charm. She always had. Always.

From the earliest childhood days that she could remember, Joel Trucker had been present in her life. The familiar smell of his musky deodorant wafted her way, and she heard him dress hurriedly and go back into the locker room. She dressed at her normal pace, spraying fresh perfume on, trademark Chanel Five, reapplying lipstick, brushing her hair, and tying it back loosely.

She stepped out of her cubicle feeling refreshed and dressed conservatively in her navy linen suit. Joel stood leaning back on the door, as if he owned the place. The crispness of his white shirt stood stark against his tanned skin. Determined not to let his presence unnerve her, she walked quickly toward him, then stopped as he spoke her name.

"My God Marcia, you are truly beautiful."

Disregarding his compliment, she simply asked, "Joel, would you please unlock the door and let me out?"

"Not yet."

She couldn't quite read his face. She was out of practice. Once upon a time, she could have grasped every nuance, gesture, grimace, sigh, and smile, and know precisely what he was thinking. Not anymore. Time had passed. So much had happened.

"Joel, please unlock the door. I'm tired. I want to do my final round and go home, it's been a busy first day."

"Busy? Are you kidding? You've seen nothing, babes. Can't you keep up with the pace? Aren't you used to doing a hard day's work? Wait until there are major emergencies, a fire in the orphanage, the odd school bus accident, then talk to me about being busy."

Ignoring his sarcasm, trying to resist the fluttering in her heart every time she looked deeply into his alert, brown eyes, Marcia stepped a little closer, and put a hand on his chest, pushing him gently toward the door. Appealingly, she implored, "let me out Joel."

"Let me in Marcia." Their eyes held unspoken words accumulated over years of longing and loathing, and leaving unsaid, what should have been said.

"Joel, please don't make my time here difficult." Their eyes locked, and she was compelled to glance away, for fear that her eyes betrayed her deepest longing. "For old times' sake, please Joel, don't make my time here hard."

Marcia was unprepared for Joel's swift reaction. He stepped away from the door and placed one foot up on the bench and leaned almost menacingly toward her. "For old times' sake? Are you serious, woman? Do you have any idea what you are asking of me?"

He didn't give her a chance to answer, but pulled her roughly into his arms, and took her mouth fully into his. Joel's grasp was powerful, it was impossible to pull away. This was no delicate, welcoming kiss. This was an all-embracing domination of Marcia's lips. She felt the demanding urgency of other parts of his body pressing her trembling frame. As quickly as he had taken her, he thrust her aside.

"Don't you ever do that to me again," Marcia said slowly, deliberately, forcibly, as if she meant it. She didn't know what she meant. The kiss had thrilled and repulsed her.

"Why would I ever want to kiss you again? I like a woman

who responds, who isn't as hard as nails and as cool as ice. You've become an Ice Maiden, Marcia, someone I hardly recognise." He walked silently to the door, unlocked it, nodded to her, and she went to walk out. "Oh, by the way," he said as he grasped her hand, "congratulations, you did superbly today. We make a great team."

Marcia quickly looked in the mirror to make sure her lipstick wasn't smudged, then walked out, fighting the tears rushing to her eyes. Joel's dominating kiss had unleashed a host of complicated, trapped emotions and desires that had lain dormant for too long. She wasn't used to emotional confusion in her professional life. She didn't like it one little bit.

She did her first hospital round in a flustered state. The children would not detect her anxiety. To them, she was the beautiful doctor with a cute pussycat badge, and kind blue eyes, that watched them carefully as she listened to their fears and stories, and reassured their parents who were visiting.

Inside, she was a torrent of raging emotions. She could do nothing to stop the image of this big handsome man with the sensual gesture of sliding his hand through his unruly curls. How dare he presume the gap of years of absence between them would mean nothing? It wasn't possible to take off where he had left off when they were considerably younger. How dare he kiss her. How dare he take her with such powerful, sexual force. He set her alive in a way she wasn't ready to admit to anyone, not even to herself.

Marcia just wanted to go home, have a long bath, prepare something easy to eat, listen to some calming Mozart and crawl into bed. Grateful that the long first day was over, she went to her workstation to gather her briefcase. A spring came back into her stride as she walked down the corridor toward the exit. Just as she was about to step outside into the heat of the day, a man stepped out of the shadows. She groaned inside her. Was there to be no peace?

"Marcia, we have to talk."

"Joel, go away, let me be. Please, I'm tired, I'm going home."

"Marcia, we'll be working closely, we can't have any tension between us."

"There's no professional tension. As you already said, we make a good team. You're right, we do, and that's all there is to it. Goodnight."

This wasn't enough for Joel. He grabbed her arm to stop her stalking off. "There is tension between us Marcia, major friction. I can feel it. I see it in your face, every time I look your way." She held his eyes.

"There is no unnecessary tension. We can do our work together as professionals, that's all that matters. And at the end of the day, we'll walk away, separately."

"You always were able to cut me off like that when you wanted to." He clicked his fingers. "You're an icicle, Marcia. A Doctor Ice Maiden. I'm human. I like to touch and feel warmth. There are many important things we need to talk about. You know that." This time, Marcia looked away, unable to admit that he might be right.

For now, Marcia was too tired to argue. She shook her head, and stalked off in haste to her flash, red Jaguar, not looking back at the weary, little, battered car parked beside her. The car brought back countless memories. Mostly, they were wonderful recollections of fun days of innocence. Why hadn't she recognised it this morning?

Was she ready to face memories again? Not if they made her think of Joel. But weren't there many good ones as well?

3

The first week of work set a clear pattern. Marcia rose early and dressed in something smart but plain. She wore no make-up other than red lipstick. Long, hot days in the north of Australia had discouraged her from bothering. Working under warm surgery lights didn't help. The few times she had worn make-up to work, it had smeared, and been streaky at the end of surgery. She no longer bothered.

Besides, she wasn't trying to impress anyone else, was she? She asked herself this question as she put on her one concession to feminine glamour, lipstick. Of course, she was not trying to impress anyone she told herself abruptly, not giving herself the luxury of time to ponder.

Time wasn't something she had in abundance. Her days were extremely busy. Somehow, her exotic, red car always sidled beside a dilapidated, old, white, Volkswagen beetle. Or this old car managed to slide in beside hers, the moment she parked. She kept reminding herself to ask Joel why he still drove such a beat-up car, but the occasion never arose.

The team of twelve met early to review the previous day's patients, and to summarise the day's activities. They then went their respective ways, and she spent most of the day working alongside of Joel, discussing the immediate needs of the patients. Morning tea was non-existent, and lunch was squashed somewhere in-between schedules, eaten in haste at a shared table with other team members, or sometimes, not eaten at all.

Every time she was near Joel, Marcia's body tingled in anticipation. Eagerness of what, she was not certain, but his mere presence excited her, making her body feel alive again as it hadn't felt for ages.

Each day, after surgery, Marcia and Joel showered before they went on their final hospital rounds of the day. However, unlike the first memorable day, medical staff from other surgical teams were using the change rooms on these occasions, and nothing private or personal had happened since that first day and the one significant, disturbing kiss. Marcia hid her disappointment when she saw other staff enter. Surely, they could time their surgery differently.

The memory of that one fierce kiss had stirred something unsettling in Marcia. Repeatedly, as she prepared for work, as she awaited seeing Joel, as she drove home after a busy day, the reality of the kiss returned to haunt her, in the most pleasant way possible. She mentally rehearsed its sensation, taste, and effect racing through her. One kiss. Just the one kiss. How could it have such an impact?

It was as if her past was returning full cycle, but not quite, it could never return as before. Too much had happened. Too much had changed. She was no longer the same woman, although she thought he was probably the same man, still gorgeous looking, sensual, charismatic, commanding, loved by all.

Daily, Joel managed to contrive his exits at the same time as she did, and they walked to their respective cars together. Their chat was trivial, sparse, never intimate. On Wednesday and Thursday, Una went home with him, and Marcia watched them laughing easily, comfortable with an occasional linked arm, and extremely relaxed in each other's presence.

Marcia assumed they were a couple. How else could you giggle and whisper and touch so easily if you weren't a couple? She watched them in her rear vision mirror, a small pang of envy creeping into her chest, or was it seeping into her heart? The pain was not simply in watching Joel and Una drive off together, it was the idea of having a man to go home with, someone to share the day's activities, and mull over trivial details. Did this happen? Did that happen?

She had lived the life of a hermit for too long. Even to think like this, was a signal, that strange things were happening to her. She would let them happen, not think too much about them. For once, she'd go with the flow. Or at least, she'd try to.

These changes swirling around inside made her think of the conversation she had had with her father recently. He was right. He kept urging her to get a social life, to contact friends she had not seen for years, to enjoy life a bit more. She kept reassuring him that she loved her work, and that was all that she needed. He was no fool. He had been the senior paediatric consultant surgeon of the same hospital his daughter now worked in. There weren't many women doctors in his day. He told her that the few who had practiced with him were unmarried women who remained as spinsters.

With reluctance, he had accepted that women's work practices are changing, and that many married women had studied medicine, and child-care was now available, but he worried about his daughter's career. He had told her that he didn't like her leaving home too young to study interstate, but she had gone anyway. He hated her facing catastrophic events so young in her life, and to cope with the tragedy, she had moved far away from family and friends, hardly communicating with anyone, returning now to her home city, but throwing herself into her work, not leaving time for socialising, or energy to talk about her trauma.

Marcia's father kept reminding his daughter of how important it is to relax, take leisure time, enjoy smelling the roses, and build up meaningful friendships. He heeded his own advice which kept him youthful and sane since the death of his darling wife. He made sure that his life was full of friendships and family connections, and he was grateful that he could still play golf reasonably well.

Marcia was thinking of her father's advice as she parked the car in the hospital car park. Today was Friday, and she planned to visit him for dinner, relax by his pool, and perhaps barbecue some fish with him. She knew that he would love this. Today, there was no white Volkswagen car beside her, and she pretended to look for something behind her, hoping that it would arrive while she scrummaged around. It did.

Marcia got out. Her cream, classic dress suited her. Its no-frills style highlighted the blondness of her hair. She watched Joel unravel his long legs, and emerge from the old car like an Amazon, broad and impressive, with the sun picking up the reddish glint in his dark hair.

"Damn," she muttered to herself. "Una is with him. She must have slept the night at his place." It shouldn't have bothered her, but it did. Terribly. Irrationally. She stormed off ahead, throwing a coolly curt, "good morning," over her shoulder.

Nothing seemed to annoy Joel, unduly. He caught up with her and grasped her arm. "Slow down Dr Knight, what's the rush on this bright, lovely Friday morning?"

Pulling away from him, smoothing down her already smooth dress, she gave him a withering glare, and pranced off alone, not that she was in any more of a hurry than her colleagues. She just couldn't cope with her contradictory emotions. Here she was telling herself that she didn't care about Joel. But she admitted that she was jealous of Una's closeness to him, and she jumped to a hasty conclusion that they'd obviously spent the night together. Yet, she was angry at herself for being so emotionally affected by Dr Joel Trucker. These mixed emotions were confusing.

No one in their right mind would deny the man's unbelievable looks, he could sign up for any modelling agency, his impressive body matched his handsome face, and as for style, he had an abundance of it. Everyone recognised his charm, the way he could talk to anyone and everyone, soothe anxieties, resolve petty disputes, and make everyone feel important. None of this meant it had to stir her emotions so intensely that her pulse raced every time she saw him. And she was a doctor. Keeping steady pulses was part of her job.

There were no exceptions to the effect his charisma invoked. In his presence, she was less articulate than normal, and she felt a stirring of passions that she had forgotten she was capable of feeling. It felt good.

Was she ready to explore these conflicting emotions? She doubted it. Too readily, she could remember the part that Joel had played in the most traumatic experience of her life. One incident she still hadn't recovered from.

The atmosphere in today's surgery was a little more tense than usual. There were some long and difficult operations, and it had been a demanding week.

At a late lunch, she had a sense that Joel wanted to say something private to her, but there was a constant movement of people about them, and the opportunity didn't arise. They went to scrub up for their last operation for the week.

Marcia slowed down as she could hear Joel's banter and sounds of laughter with others behind her, as they deviated off into their separate ways. Marcia slipped quietly into the preparation room and was engrossed in her cleansing tasks of scrubbing up. She turned around in a startled state as she felt a large warm hand on her back, and a familiar voice whisper, "my beautiful helper."

"Helper?" she asked, extreme annoyance written all over her solemn face, and loud as a bell in the tone of her voice. "I am not here to help you. I am here to help the patient."

Unusually, he didn't argue further. With a more serious look than usual, and knowing he couldn't touch her while she was preparing herself with sterilised items, he asked quietly, "Marcia, would you come out for a meal with me tonight?"

"No," she replied tightly.

"Why not?" His hurt was evident. Pain lined his dear face.

"I've other things planned."

"With another man?"

"That's right," she answered, not letting him know that the man was her father.

They worked in the theatre surgery with a busy determination. She felt a certain strain between them, more deliberate than usual. Joel was very careful to walk around pieces of medical equipment to avoid brushing against her. She had enjoyed his occasional touch. It made her feel part of the team, more particularly, part of Doctor Joel Trucker's team.

Joel was a naturally affectionate man, hugging in a kindly, brotherly way, an arm around staff shoulders when they needed encouragement. He was the oldest son in a large family and being demonstrative to others was the way he'd been brought up. It was never inappropriate. No one misinterpreted it as offensive and certainly not as any harassment.

Today, his physical distancing made Marcia feel isolated. It also made her want him more. Was this his tactic? Was he devious? She hadn't remembered that being a character trait. Usually, he was straightforward, clear as a crystal ocean.

The precise moment she asked herself these hard questions, she caught his eye watching her watching their patient, as she looked up briefly, and he waited an unusually long moment for Una to hand him a different scalpel. Probably, it was only a second longer than usual.

What a power of a look! What were those deep brown eyes

saying to her across his masked face? Anything? What did she want them to say? Why was she always so cold in her responses? She didn't mean to be. Was she really an Ice Maiden? She was incredibly offended when he called her this horrible name. Surely, she hadn't always been cold and abrupt? Indeed, she knew that he knew otherwise. That was in the past.

Almost as if Marcia had anticipated it, she and Joel, the man of her confused musings, were the last ones in the theatre today. No other medical staff needed the change rooms. It was Friday. Staff were keen for their weekend getaway. Marcia caught herself walking down toward the change room with Joel, but then she remembered that while he needed to have a quick chat to the patients he had operated on, there was no surgery for them on Saturday, so she didn't need to go and review new patients.

Her mind raced confusedly. Why was she making such an issue of nothing? However, she confessed that she wanted to be locked away in this room again, with only Joel for company. He sensed this and plonked down on a bench.

"You look tired," Marcia said kindly.

"Yes, I'm looking forward to a weekend to recuperate."

Silence hovered as Marcia had visions of Joel and Una romping about in relaxed glee. But she remembered that he'd asked her out. This was confusing. Recognising it was not her business, she asked, "what do you have planned for the weekend?"

She shouldn't have bothered, quick as a flash, he responded, "oh, nothing much, just a wild, orgy, my darling."

Marcia looked embarrassed. "Oh, I'll just quickly get changed then and escape."

"Escape for a key part of my plans you mean?" They sat opposite each other, wary, weary, but satisfied in knowing that they had fulfilled an excellent first week of work, and that they could work cooperatively together, despite the emotional friction they experienced. They were good at disguising this tension to others. No one picked up on it or questioned them.

Marcia wondered what was going through his clever mind as his eyes never left her body. She couldn't look beautiful, not in the green gown over her formless, white surgical dress, no make-up, her hair messy after pulling her cap off roughly. It was impossible. Yet the intensity of his gaze unnerved her.

"Why do you look at me like that?"

He deliberately shifted his eyes to look slowly from her long legs upward, pausing to imagine her body in shapely clothes, letting his eyes roam up to her breasts, not very noticeable under the gown, hovering at her full mouth, returning to her eyes, and fixing his gaze there. She held his gaze.

"Marcia, you are quite beautiful," he said quietly, and with clear meaning.

"Hardly," she said as she looked down at her gowns.

Joel stood up, shut the door, but didn't lock it. Marcia too stood up, anticipating longingly, a repeat, memorable kiss. Strangely, Joel stood on a bench, high above her, and placed his hands on her shoulders and gently drew her to him. She nestled softly into his stomach for a few seconds, relishing the familiar intimacy of touch, and moved away, going to her locker to get her clothes.

"Marcia, I know I keep repeating myself, but we do need to talk. Soon. How about now?"

"You keep restating this, I keep saying, we're doing fine."

"You might be, but I'm not."

"That's what has to be."

"You mean if you're okay, it doesn't matter about me." It was more of a statement than a question.

"That's not what I mean." She looked fiery, although she didn't mean to. She hoped it was better than looking icy.

"Well, that's what it amounts to."

Marcia shrugged. "Then, that's life."

"Spoiled little rich girl, huh?"

"Don't throw me that line again. You can't be doing too bad for yourself. I'm sure my dad has made sure you've not gone without anything you need."

"Don't give me that line. What kind of car do you drive? Remind me?"

"You obviously choose to keep the old VW."

"What would you know about me anymore, Marcia? Why do you treat me like this, as if we're strangers? Hugging you in the sandpit is my first memory. I think I was three." His face expressed a sad anger, a conspicuous disappointment about their relationship. "How can you wipe the past away, as if it never existed? It did. And I've been a big part of it."

This was not territory Marcia wanted to enter. "Who knows why any of us do what we do? The past is past." Her response was trite.

Joel stepped down from the bench and stood so that she couldn't move. "Why do you play the cold, callous icy woman, Marcy? What have I ever done against you?"

Her heart was racing. His patience intimidated yet thrilled her. But with his question, her face convulsed into enraged features. "Don't call me that old endearment," she hissed slowly between closed teeth, ignoring his question.

"Why not, Marcy?" Joel deliberately repeated the pet name, knowingly provocative only to them, as he came across to her and cradled her face with a warm hand either side of each cheek. He brought his mouth down to a breath away from hers, and mockingly asked, "why not, Marcy? Maybe the endearment will remind you that you're a woman with feelings, passion, a body, and maybe even a warm, beating heart. Melt Doctor Ice Maiden, melt. Melt for me."

At this moment, Marcia was very aware of being a woman with feelings and cravings in a sexually starved body. Through the looseness of their gowns, she could feel the hardness of his body. Pressed against him, her breasts felt like putty waiting to be moulded. She smelt his familiar musk, mixing with her Chanel Five, and she wanted to pull him tightly to her, to convince him that she was a sensual, desirous, and desirable woman. She was warm, not a block of ice. Her hands felt wild, wanting to explore up his gown and to convince him she was not an Ice Maiden. At this moment in time, she would have yielded to any of his demands, so great was her desire.

She was also good at disguise. She had had years of practice in suppressing her emotions, squashing them away in a tight, little box. Her face gave nothing away, but she couldn't hide from him forever. Once upon a time, he had known almost everything there was to know about her.

Instead of responding with any intimacy, Joel walked away, grabbed his clothes and toiletries bag from his locker, and walked into the shower cubicle. Marcia disguised her disappointment. There would be no second kiss.

Marcia threw off her gowns, and deciding not to shower, she changed quickly. She left, throwing a hasty, "see you next week, Joel," over her shoulder, as if he meant absolutely nothing to her at all. This was the first time she had walked out of the exit door without the reassuring presence of Doctor Trucker beside her, or a comforting step away. She didn't need him to hold her hand. Did she? Was she kidding herself?

It was a very hot afternoon. She couldn't keep putting off her father's almost daily request to visit him. He'd started pleading to her. Dear man, he missed her so much. Marcia stopped off at a local supermarket, did the small amount of grocery shopping she needed, went home to change into a long, cream, silk, wrap-over skirt with a matching singlet top. There was no need for anything warmer. She listened to the weekend forecast as she started to unwind. It was going to be a hot weekend, very hot.

She threw her black bikini into a bag, looking forward to diving into her father's pool. He was a bit old-fashioned and preferred a woman to be in a one-piece bathing costume, but Marcia had been so tired of always having to wear a conservative swimming costume as a girl, then as a teenager, and even sometimes as a young woman, that now she was a career woman, she wore nothing but bikinis. Her choice.

Unusually jauntily, she left her apartment, anticipating a carefree evening. To her horror, as she began the steep incline to her father's prestigious property, she saw an old, beaten up, white Volkswagen sitting at the top of the drive as if it owned the world, there, in the exact position where she normally parked. She had no intention of driving home, her father would never have forgiven her. He had started to beg her to visit him, pricking her hard conscience.

But there were some things she would never share with her father, no matter how close they were, and her mixed feelings toward Joel came into this category. Perhaps if her mother was alive, things may have been different. She would have welcomed confiding to her mother. But her mother was no longer here. No one could take her place. She was gone. She missed her loving face with a heartbreaking yearning.

If she was thinking straight, she might have anticipated this happening, but why had Joel not mentioned it to her? Was he trying to trick her? Of course, he was. He probably knew all along that she was coming to see her father. Maybe her father had even told him. Nothing would surprise her. They were incredibly close. What would she find when she went inside? Her heart fluttered erratically.

4

In fact, there was nothing unusual about seeing the Volkswagen sitting at the top of the drive, except that it was sitting in her parking position. Hers. Joel had been coming to their house since he was a toddler, first of all in his mother's trusty car.

Then, he gained his driving license straight after high school, and having saved every coin possible to purchase his first car. From an early age, he tutored children in science subjects, as well as racing about doing newspaper deliveries. In summer, he taught surfing skills to rich kids whose parents could pay the vast amounts he set. The day he purchased this car was a highlight of his youth. He adored the car and had looked after it carefully. He knew exactly where Marcia usually parked. He had pushed his way in. Uninvited.

My word, they had had such youthful adventures in his first car! Much of their growing up together revolved around the car. What stories it could tell! Joel treasured it and had a local mechanic look after the engine regularly. It was as if Joel and his car were part of Marcia's family's property, and even in that minimal way, he was part of her life. Until she walked away, making sure that he was no longer part of her life. He was back in it, but what part would he play? What part did she want him to play?

Their mothers had shared a love for bushwalking and had first met when they joined a women's walking group. Since early days of married life, they formed a close friendship. It was a curious relationship. Marcia's mother Patricia was the wealthy wife of a successful surgeon Bill, who doted on their only child. Joel's mother Myra was a poor, but contented wife of a struggling builder Sam, who only just managed to keep financially afloat.

Joel was one of a large family. As the oldest child, he had learnt to take responsibility early in life. Often, his parents left him in charge of his five younger siblings. Sometimes, there was only just enough food placed on the table for the seven in the family. They shared everything they had. Despite the class differences and enormous variations in lifestyles, the two women forged a close bond, and Patricia and Myra never let money or status come between their lovely, warm relationship. Also, Patricia was sensitive enough to know when to drop a bit more food over to her friend's house in such a relaxed way that it never made her friend feel awkward or in debt. This was a beautiful gift her mother had, one of her many wonderful gifts of generosity.

Patricia was only able to have one child. There had been complications at childbirth, and she accepted with gratitude her one healthy daughter. Bill, Marcia's father, took to Joel from the day he was born. From the moment he set eyes on the small child, it was as if he was his son, a son to be shared with Myra and Sam. He loved watching Joel and Marcia play together in his spacious backyard. From the time when Joel started school, Bill told him that one day he'd become a great surgeon, like he was. As he nurtured Joel in this belief, the young boy took it for granted that it was a possibility, despite the family's material poverty, and neither parent having gone to university.

Bill talked constantly to this young lad and to his young daughter, about studying medicine, lending them medical textbooks even before they went to medical school. He let them handle his medical instruments, and instructed them in basic stethoscope usage from childhood days. They had listened to each other's hearts beating for as long as they could remember. They knew the sound and feel of their heartbeats. They were in rhythm. Back then, it seemed like a game. Now, who knows?

When the time came, even though Joel and Marcia had won scholarships to medical school, Bill assisted Joel financially, in the same way that he assisted his daughter through university. He did this in such an unobtrusive, undemanding way, that it was almost as if Joel was doing him a favour by accepting the gifts.

Bill took it for granted that one day, Joel would marry his daughter, not in return for everything that he'd done for him, but that it was in their best interests. Of course, they must love each other. They'd played at being mummies and daddies, and doctors and nurses, and then as doctors and doctors since they could walk.

Bill's dream had not seen fruition. Life hadn't worked out as the fairy story he had hoped for. He wished he could wave a magic wand over this young couple who he loved so dearly.

Marcia had been away for so long now, that it was peculiar to have these childhood memories flash back in haste. She stood at the top of the drive, reminiscing. As a child, then as a teenager, she hadn't thought twice about them, they were just the facts of her life, and therefore, also part of Joel's life. He was that much part of her life story. There were few aspects of growing up where he didn't feature strongly. He was part of the furniture, so to speak. He moved in and out of the house, like he belonged there. He was probably more comfortable in her old home than Marcia was at this stage of her life.

With a heavy reluctance, she walked into her childhood home as if she was suddenly a stranger. She deposited her freshly purchased fish in the fridge and peered out of the kitchen window onto the slate-paved patio. She saw two good-looking men deep in conversation, laughing boisterously. It was time to join them.

Her father caught sight of her and jumped up as quickly as his ageing body would allow. "Marcia, my darling daughter, you visit your old dad at last!" and he embraced her lovingly. "Isn't it great that I've got my surrogate son to visit me, or I would be a very lonely old man," he teased her. He was also chastising her gently, Marcia understood this, and dropped her head briefly in shame.

Marcia didn't know where to look. Joel sat in nothing but his tight, brief bathers, every bodily bulge conspicuous. He was well endowed and did nothing to disguise his impressive body. He knew her well enough to see that she was uncomfortable with his exposure, and curiously, this pleased him. Sitting on a towel, his body glistened with moisture, clearly, he had just come out of the pool.

They had swum together in this pool thousands of times, she had seen him looking like this countless times before. Why was it bothering her now? Why was she restless? He was affecting her emotions with a crazy, frenzied desire.

"My God man, do you have to flick your hair like that?" Marcia asked herself, irate that every occasion he did so, it stirred her passions. Nothing had stirred her for ages. It felt strange, but she welcomed the sensations.

"Hello Joel," she simply said, somewhat icily. He grinned, relishing her discomfort.

"Well come on Marcia, get your bathers on," her dad encouraged. "Joel's been telling me about what a busy week you've had. You go in and have a swim with Joel, and I'll get the barbecue started. Did you get that fish I asked for?" She nodded.

Her father was right. There were times when a conservative one-piece costume would be preferable to a low-cut, underwired, high-leg bikini. She went coyly into the outside changing room, looked in the mirror, and thought that the only thing she could do was to dive into the pool as quickly as possible -- so she did. Marcia swam a few lengths expertly and stopped at the far edge of the pool. She didn't have to look where he was, she felt his eyes boring into her body, now glistening with moisture and sunlight. Bill had tactfully disappeared on the pretext of preparing food.

Joel dived into the pool, swimming the full-length underwater. She knew it was childish and churlish to swim away, so she waited to see what he'd do. Joel swam up to her, grasped her ankles, ran his hand up her leg, and then up her thigh, grabbed her waist with two hands, then came up for air. With his left hand tucked into the elastic of her high-cut leg, his right fingers dropped into her full cleavage, and stroked up and down. She was breathing deeply, conscious of her firm breasts moving up and down at his eye level. This man was enjoying watching their beauty.

It had been many years since she had let anyone touch her like this, and looking into her eyes, Joel knew that she was being transported back in time. They'd enjoyed many good times together – times that had been horribly disrupted.

His hands came up to grasp the flimsy cloth covering her breasts, and just as he began to explore, desperately trying to feel her flesh, she broke free, and began swimming crazily up and down the pool, like an Olympic athlete possessed by the image of the gold medal. It was nearly in her grasp. She had to win it. She simply had to. Would she?

Anyone who observed her behaviour, might have guessed the sexual energy that was being released with every turn at the end of the pool. No matter how frantically she swam, she was aware of his body stretched languorously in the water, moving slowly above the surface to watch this gorgeous, sexy mermaid with a thin black strap across her back and shoulders, and a mere skimpy pair of briefs to cover her bottom.

Under the water, every time she flipped over to do another lap, Marcia saw a long pair of muscular legs and an enormous broad chest and back, well-covered with glistening hair. She still liked manly hair, she never could relate to these young fitness freaks who waxed their bodies, it didn't seem quite right to her. What she could never take her eyes off, was the brief bathers that covered his manly parts. The sight was driving her crazy. She wanted to swim over and rip his bathers off, and tear her bikini from her body, and entangle her body with his, and let his tongue find every part of her sensuous body that she had covered up for too long.

How many times had they swum in this pool together? Countless times! This time felt different. Ripples of energy ran up and down the lanes. She was the electric current.

Bill came outside with the food to place on the barbecue. Marcia climbed out of the pool, used the outdoor shower, and changed back into her clothes. She pulled her hair back into a sparkly clasp. Joel sat watching her as she came out of the changing room.

"Some energy you have Marcia after such a week like we've had," he laughed. She blushed.

"Works you hard, does he?" called Bill.

"Dad, I don't work for Joel, remember," she retorted, glaring at him.

But her father was still old-fashioned. Very old-school. He remembered what it was like in his day. "But the surgeon is always in control, he's the one in charge."

"There's no hierarchies any more, Bill," reassured Joel, ever calming of any potential conflict that might erupt, "we work as a team."

"A close team, some closer than others," taunted Marcia, remembering his ability to alienate her in the surgical theatre, merely by bodily distance, and recalling his physical ease with Una.

Joel threw a colourful shirt over his broad shoulders, and pulled on some board shorts, noticing with a smile every time Marcia's wrap-over skirt blew open in the gentle breeze, exposing her leg, and wincing inwardly every time she drew back to cover her leg.

The two men chatted easily, mainly about how hospitals and surgical techniques are changing. Bill loved to hear of new medical advances. Marcia was grateful not to be included in this discussion. It wasn't that she was excluded, she simply chose to listen rather than to participate. There was too much racing around her mind, particularly to do with the handsome man sitting there beside her father, as if it was the most natural thing in the world. In many ways, it was.

But enough had happened to change that. Joel might be able to disregard the past, but she could not. Her mind flittered there daily.

Marcia's equilibrium was shattered, as she saw her father turn to her, and ask, "so, when are you two going to make me the happiest man in the world?"

Marcia knew exactly what he was referring to, and evasively replied, "I am Daddy. I'm working in your old hospital, just as you wanted me to do. And Joel's got your old job. What more could a man wish for?"

Keen for some sport, Joel prompted, "now Bill, is that what you meant?" He knew this man deeply.

Bill was wired up now, he'd drunk a few beers. He rarely drunk during the week. He only drunk at social occasions, and to have a laugh with others. "No Joel, it wasn't what I mean, my girl works too hard. Now, come on my dears. It's time to make me a happy man."

"You are a happy man. Dad, let life be, I'm not a girl, remember?"

"No darling, yes darling, well, you're certainly not a boy." He was trying to be funny, it didn't work. The man paused, and with emotion in his voice, said, "life doesn't keep on."

"What's wrong?" his daughter asked concerned, "is there something wrong with you?"

"Not at all dear, I'm fit as a fiddle. It's just that particularly since your mother's passing, I'm reminded how much life is for living, and I'm convinced that you are not living life to the full."

"What changes do you think she should make, Bill?" Joel persisted, eyeing a full exposure of leg that Marcia was too anxious to bother to cover.

"Joel, forget it." She glared at him.

"Now Marcia, Joel has asked a valid question. You have to put your past behind you, you too Joel, move into the future, both of you, move together."

"I have," said Joel quietly, and with a passionate voice, continued, "I'm waiting for Marcia to enter the real world of the present, as well, before she even contemplates the future."

Marcia stood up angrily. It was as if the penny had just dropped. "Dad, did you know that Joel had moved back to Sydney?"

"Of course, I did. You know that he's like a son to me. He's never lost contact with me, the way you have. He keeps in close communication with me. He phones me, writes amusing letters, drops in regularly, cooks for me, he does all the things that good sons do." His voice expressed gratitude to his surrogate son. But underlying this, was the implicit disappointment he felt that over the years, Marcia had kept away from him. There was no condemnation in his tone. Only grief. He adored his daughter. But he missed her presence. Deeply. "What's your problem, my darling daughter?" he asked, seriously bewildered, and very concerned.

"Did you never think that I might not have moved back, had I known?"

"Yes," he answered honestly, "that's exactly what I thought your stubborn response would be if I told you." There was a terrible sadness in his voice. "That's exactly why I didn't tell you. And, when you took on your mother's maiden name, I assumed that Joel wouldn't pick up on that because he didn't mention anything to me about your return. Fate has brought you two together again. I am sure of it, I am quite sure." The old man gazed away. "Destiny takes us places we never dream of travelling ourselves."

"I'll live my life my way thanks." Marcia looked at her father, the man she loved intensely, but who at this precise moment, annoyed her for wanting her to have what she could not have. She couldn't have it, wasn't that, right? Was it?

She then looked intensely at Joel, the man who stirred sexual passion in her that she'd long thrust aside. She grabbed her bag, kissed her father dutifully, and without a glance at Joel, left the table.

Marcia ignored her father's cry, "but you can't leave. You haven't eaten any of the gorgeous fish that you brought." She heard his cry, heard the sadness in his voice, but walked on, determinedly alone.

Marcia drove home in haste, threw herself onto her bed fully clothed, and cried tears of bewilderment, falling fitfully into sleep. Her last thought before dropping into sleep was "is there really something called destiny?" In her mind, she heard her father's words, "Destiny takes us places we never dream of travelling ourselves." Where was destiny taking her?

5

Sunshine streamed into Marcia's bedroom. She stretched her long legs, noticing in disbelief her crumpled silk clothes. A noise had woken her. Was she hearing things? Was that her apartment speaker ringing again? She stumbled across to it.

"Who's there?" she asked into the speaker box.

"Morning Marcia my darling, can I come in?"

Marcia groaned at the familiar sound of Joel's voice. Would he never leave her alone? Was that what she wanted? Surely not. She looked down at her dishevelled appearance. "It's a bit early, isn't it?"

"Do I have to stand out here and talk, or would you press your buzzer and let me in? Please?" Joel asked with humour in his tone, as well as authority.

Not knowing what she was doing, Marcia pressed the buzzer that released the front door to her apartment block. She took a quick glance at herself in the hall mirror and groaned. Did it matter?

Joel walked in looking fresh and casual in shorts, smart tee-shirt, and clean white sports trainers.

"How did you know which apartment I lived in, where it is for that matter?"

Joel rolled his eyes. "Do you really think I didn't know where you live? Your father is falling over himself to tell me anything and everything I want to know about you?"

"Well, what do you want at this early hour of the morning?" Her voice was gruff.

"Early? Are you kidding?" he grinned.

Marcia looked at the hall clock in disbelief. It said eleven o'clock, and then she felt stupid. Clearly, the first week of work had left her exhausted, emotionally as well as physically. "I had no idea of the time."

Joel came over to her, and slid his hand over the silk fabric, finding the split in her wrap-over skirt. He said nothing about the fact that she clearly had slept in it. His hand slipped up a thigh, and she squirmed a little, unsure what to do. She remembered that she had thrown her lace panties off before going to sleep. He discovered this fact quickly, and she shoved his hand away, despite craving its touch. "Do you mind?" and she pulled away, pretending to be annoyed. She loved the feel of his hand there. She wanted it to stay, to roam further.

"Have it your way Marcia, you always did, but you're simply delaying the inevitable."

Marcia despised it when men presumed to know her mind's intentions with her body. At this stage, she didn't even know as much herself. She was embarrassed by her slept-in appearance. Feeling awkward, she asked, "why are you here Joel?"

"To take you out, to talk, to get to know each other anew, shall I go on? How about brunch and a swim at the beach?"

"It's too hot for the beach."

"You've changed, you always loved the beach, whatever the weather. It's never too hot for the beach, or too cold for that matter. The ocean soothes my soul."

"I keep telling you that I've changed, but you won't listen." She stood aloof, taking him in fully. Clearly, he was pleased by his outrageous gesture of calling uninvited on a fiercely hot Saturday morning. It wasn't that astonishing. They were old friends. But that was in the past.

Ignoring the nonsense idea that he wasn't the one listening, good-naturedly, he said, "fine, let's have a long brunch, and then your father is out for the day, we could have the pool to ourselves."

"You know my dad's movements that intimately, do you?"

"Someone has to take care of him," he responded, somewhat accusingly, holding her eyes without a flicker.

For one moment, she felt ashamed, she had no idea what her father's plans for the day were. The next moment, she was lashing into him again. "I don't think I could trust you in the pool with me with no one there to observe."

To this, Joel laughed heartily, and came across and took Marcia in his arms. One hand smoothed her hair off her face, the other hand slipped under her silk singlet top to find a well-rounded breast. Just once, he stroked her nipple that was peeking through the soft silky fabric. "Marcia, I think that you want me as much as I want you. I see it in your constant gaze. There is a big difference between us. I admit it, you don't."

"Joel, don't presume what you don't know." Her eyes were hard, and she pulled right away from him. He was correct. Again. As usual.

For a long while, Joel stood looking at her, his eyes moving over her top, to the nipples pushing through the creamy fabric, and then he let his eyes pause on her lips and eyes. Marcia was curious. She sensed he was working up to saying something difficult, but nothing could have prepared her for the simple finality of what he said.

Quietly, but with a fierce determination, he walked over and grabbed Marcia firmly by her shoulders. "Marcia, we have to talk."

"About what?" Marcia looked away, scared by the intensity she read in his face.

"You know what," came the obvious reply.

"No, I don't," came the evasive response.

"You do, Marcia. You're just being especially stupid."

"Stupid? Stupid?" she repeated, furious at him. "Me, stupid?" Fury appeared in her face. They had topped medical school, in some years he had received the highest grades, in the other years, he came second to her first position in different subjects.

"Yes, damn you Marcy, you're being really stupid."

"Don't call me that."

"Why not Marcy? Remind you of the night you'll never face up to, does it?"

"I have faced up to it," she said softly. She hadn't. Not fully. Not properly. Not in a way that would let her relate easily to Joel, to let her melt her iciness in his presence.

"Then talk about it with me, Marcia, please." Joel's voice was pleading, desperate for her to respond. "Marcia, I need to make sense of the gaps in our lives. I want you to talk to me about Rob and Trish."

At the mere mention of these two names, Marcia punched Joel vigorously on the arms. "Get out, get out, get out." He was a big, strong man, a few ladylike punches weren't going to distract him. Instantly, Marcia turned into a wild animal, screeching, and trying to push him out of the door. "Get out, you heartless man, get out," and now she was scratching his arms like a crazy beast. She pushed him toward the door, screaming, "you horrible man, get out. I don't want to hear those names again. I don't ever want to see you again, get out." She shoved him out of the door, and watched him stumble, then she slammed the door shut.

Marcia heard a desperate, feeble voice cry at her remote control, "please Marcia, calm down, let me explain myself. Let me tell you why I believe that we need to talk."

"Go away," she screamed hysterically, "go away, you horrid man."

He wasn't a horrible man. He was an amazingly kind doctor, a truly sensitive man. He was her oldest longtime friend. Her emotions were tumbling upside down.

Again, like the preceding night, Marcia threw herself onto her bed, crying like a crazy, possessed woman. Never had she so much wanted someone to share her sadness with, and never, had she felt so alone. Her father was out for the day and anyway, he was bound to side with Joel.

She hadn't even informed any of her past friends that she'd returned to Sydney. When she left the city, she broke contact with them, not even sending Christmas or birthday cards. She wasn't on Facebook and had no intention of joining. All that personal exposure on social media and posting endless selfies wasn't her style at all. Embarrassment about ignoring all her previous acquaintances prevented her from ringing them.

She was totally alone, except for Joel, and talking with him was impossible. This was obvious, wasn't it? Was it?

How dare the thought of talking with Joel about her woes enter her head. Joel! He was the reason for this emotional turmoil.

How dare he mention Rob and Trish, and with a reminder of these names again, Marcia thrashed about on her bed like a fish out of water, pounding her pillows with clenched fists. On her knees and palms, she buried her head on the pillow, and collapsed in a pathetic heap. Despite the heat of the day, she pulled the comforting duvet over her head, tucked herself womblike into a foetal position, and fell back into a fretful doze.

A shrill sound of the phone woke her several times, but she ignored it, and slipped back again into a stunned state of semi-sleep. Only when she heard a vigorous knocking on the door, did she stagger out to see who was rapping so persistently.

It was her next-door neighbour, a kindly, older woman whom she had politely but reservedly chatted to over the weeks of settling in. The woman was clearly alarmed at seeing the distressed state of Marcia, and promptly asked, "are you okay, my dear? Can I help?"

"No, no," blurted Marcia, highly embarrassed. "What was it you wanted?"

"Just to give you this," and she handed Marcia a small white envelope. As explanation, she added, "a man outside the apartment block begged me to hand deliver this to you." Rather conspiratorially, the neighbour said, "he's very handsome, professional looking, if you know what I mean, maybe a doctor or a lawyer. It must be very important, because he's been waiting in the sun for ages, lingering about waiting for someone to come back into the apartments, so that he could give them this envelope."

Marcia snatched the envelope with a quick "thanks," and didn't give the concerned neighbour a chance to question her further, so quickly shut the door and went back inside. As if she needed to ask who it was from, she already knew. She threw the envelope on the sofa and looked at herself in the mirror. Sheer, utter disbelief filled her. What must her neighbour think of her? She looked frightful. A total mess. Confusion hovered. Typically, she dressed immaculately and stayed in control of her emotions, avoiding all forms of excess as a principle.

The phone shattered her equilibrium. This time, she snatched her mobile.

"Yes?"

"Have you read the note?"

"No," and she threw the phone onto her bed.

Marcia walked over to the envelope as if it was dynamite, a bomb waiting to be detonated. Slowly, she tore open the envelope, pulling out the small card as if it was a pin coming out of a bomb.

Her eyes blurred as she looked slowly at the front. It was a dramatic black card with a tiny red heart in the middle. You could only just see the heart-shape. Overleaf, on the white side of the card, she read the words, "Dearest Marcia, whether you'll acknowledge it or not, we do need to talk. Working closely together at the hospital is important for us both, and we can't work professionally if there are visible tensions between us. I want to take you out for a meal. We can talk casually about the past, and I give you my promise that I won't mention those names that you can't face."

His timing was perfect. The phone rang again. Her father had insisted she put Joel's number into her phone. Seeing his name pop up on the screen, she coolly said, "yes?"

"Marcia, are you okay?"

"Brilliant," she replied sarcastically.

"Good, then how long do you need to get ready?"

"What's the time now?"

"It's five o'clock."

"It isn't, it can't be."

"Yes, it is. Why, what time did you think it was?"

Marcia hadn't realised how long she had slept, and certainly wasn't about to admit to it. Evasively, she replied, "whatever, I thought it was more like four o'clock."

"Marcia, you sound quite confused. Are you okay? Can I come over and get you?"

"I need some air to clear my head," and Marcia moved back into professional mode. This was the state of mind she excelled in. "I don't feel like any fancy meal, and I don't want to dress up." The truth was, she hadn't needed many smart clothes for her previous position in hot northern Australia, but now she needed to update her wardrobe. This was Sydney, an extremely fashionable city. "Come as you were before. Give me thirty minutes. I just want to go for a walk on the beach, and then go somewhere casual, just a café meal sitting outside."

"Fine, I'll see you in thirty minutes." Joel had no intention of giving Marcia any more time to change her mind.

In exactly thirty minutes, Marcia had showered and transformed her appearance. She wore a short, sleeveless, red shirt dress with white sandals. She drew her hair off her face with red clasps and put on a tinted moisturiser. Her red lipstick finished the transformation. Placing her Gucci sunglasses perched on her nose, she heard the buzzer, and not even bothering to answer it, she tripped down to meet Joel.

What would the rest of the day bring? Could he avoid mentioning those names again?

6

Marcia's outward appearance of light-hearted self-confidence belied the tumultuous inner beatings of her heart, which was more like an impatient bee fluttering from one flower to the next, never finding the nectar to be sufficiently satisfying. The preceding night and the messy day had left her feeling drained. She needed to be invigorated. In embarrassment, she noted several long scratch marks down Joel's arm.

He saw her looking at them and diffused her shame by grinning. "You do wear a cat badge in the wards, don't you?"

Marcia smiled accordingly. "What badge do you wear?"

"Grr, beware, I'm a lion, I'm the King of the Jungle, the King of all cats."

"Typical." She allowed a small grin.

Marcia was grateful to Joel for silence for most of the journey. It was so strange to be back in his little car. They had driven in it together countless times, they had grown up in it, it had listened to their youthful expressions of hope and despair, and witnessed many rites of passage, and had always been kind to them. For a moment, Marcia let herself be transported back to her teenage years. They were good days, uncomplicated by adult responsibilities.

As they neared the beach, she turned in the small bucket seats, her knee bumping his, and the sensation of his rough hairy leg against her smooth soft one made her squirm uncomfortably.

"What is it, Marcia? You look as if you wanted to ask me something?"

Why was he always so perceptive, acutely sensitive to her when she was most frequently rude to him? Icy in fact. "I just wanted to know why you keep this car?" Joel ignored her and kept driving. She repeated herself. "Why do you keep this car when you could easily afford to buy a new one?"

"What do you know what I can afford?"

"Don't be ridiculous. You're a senior surgeon, you must earn a lot more than me."

"Do you know why I keep this car?" He drove on silently for a while. "Because I like this car."

"Is that all?"

"Marcia, if you really stopped and thought about it, you'd realise most of the reasons why I keep this car, but clearly, I'm not allowed to talk about certain things with you." With this confession, they were back into the jungle that Marcia was too afraid to enter. The lion had spoken. She was a mere pussy cat.

The walk on the beach was pleasant. A light afternoon breeze broke the intensity of the day's heat. Marcia deliberately carried her sandals in her hand, in-between her body and Joel, so that neither hands would ever brush against each other. Every time he light-heartedly jumped onto a rock and walked the other side of her, she switched the sandals into her other hand. She didn't know why she was avoiding touch when it was what she craved. His touch.

They kept the conversation easy, on topics of their innocent childhood and light-hearted youth prior to leaving for medical school. Joel didn't disclose any of his suppressed jealousy of the ease of life that Marcia's wealthy background had afforded her, while he did paper rounds from boyhood, then swimming instruction every school holiday as a young man, and then throughout University, he'd tutored high school students in biology. He earnt money for the extra things he needed in life, like medical textbooks, and of course, the upkeep for his precious car. He always sent his parents a special present for their birthdays. Bill's generous gifts had come as life savers.

Today, as they drove in this old, familiar car, both were lost in their thoughts of the past. Marcia didn't remind him of how annoyed she always was, with both their parents' assumptions that one day, in the sweet bye-and-bye, they would eventually marry.

Instead, they kept conversation on safe territory, laughing at the idea that as children they had played doctors and nurses, as well as doctors and doctors, and then all the little silly *faux pas* they had made as teenagers at school dances, pool parties, and eventually at driving lessons. From as long as they could remember, they had always been together. Always. Any time the topic seemed to head back toward university days and their social life there, they smartly cut it back again to their youth. Safe territory, the only one to be in, at this precarious moment in life.

Slowly, Marcia felt some of the day's tensions disappear. Joel was such a good companion. Indeed, she'd almost forgotten how good-natured a friend he was to be with. Their easy discussions reminded her of how much they'd shared together, how much they had in common. Yet, there was a big gap in their lives where he knew nothing of her life, and she knew nothing about his current life.

The safest way to broach this topic without being too awkward or devious, was to ask about their past mutual friends. However, to do so, would by implication force them to re-enter a social circle that very deliberately, for their own reasons, they had both chosen to escape from.

Marcia knew Joel closely enough to know that he wouldn't live his life as a hermit, as she had. He was always popular, as captain of sports teams, prefect at school, the much-desired man at school dances, a central focus of attention at parties, and the life and soul of social gatherings. A week at the hospital had already shown her that none of his charm had dissipated. To the contrary, with extra maturity, his magnetism flowed over into his professional career. That was some achievement she acknowledged. Surely, he must have contacted some of his friends again. Were they also her friends? Still? Could they be? Did she want them to be?

Marcia began to probe him about the whereabouts of some of their mutual acquaintances. "Were they married? Who was divorced? What profession did they pursue? Did they have children? Were they happy, or not?" she asked of certain names, but not others. The absences were stark. He grasped this. Sensibly, he let her ask the questions.

Precisely, factually, without elaborating, Joel filled her in on those past mutual friends that he did know about. He kept to the ones that were safe to talk about. They walked back to the car. Not once, had Joel touched Marcia, neither accidentally nor casually. Marcia wasn't sure whether to be relieved or disappointed, she suspected the latter. Why didn't she know? She was usually totally in control of her feelings. Or perhaps she hadn't let her feelings surface over these last years, so that she had quite forgotten what it was like to express passionate feelings for anyone. Of course, she wanted him to touch her.

Suddenly, she realised she was very hungry. In fact, she hadn't eaten a bite all day, so she was relieved when Joel suggested that it was time to eat.

He drove for a few minutes to an area that seemed uncannily familiar to Marcia, yet simultaneously, astonishingly different. It was a street filled with small cosmopolitan cafés. Many of them had outdoor settings, just as she had hoped for. Multicultural Australia sat outside, enjoying the balmy evening, eating all varieties of culinary delights. In between the cafés, were tiny bookshops with windy staircases, specialist boutiques selling only the sort of garments that the very bravest or trendiest people would dare to wear. One day, she'd look at them, not quite yet.

Joel drove down the long, tree-lined street, and parked at the bottom of the road so they'd have to wander back up and down its full length. He unravelled his large frame quickly, raced around to Marcia's side of the car, and opened the door flamboyantly.

"There we go, my dear lady. I am at your service."

Marcia returned a glazed stare and started walking slowly up the street, looking frantically around her. A frightened look came across her face, she desperately looked left and right, forward, and backward, as if she was looking at a war-torn scene of destruction rather than an upmarket, interesting street full of quaint shops and cafés, filled with fascinating people enjoying themselves.

She paused beside an enormous ghost gum tree, its branches reaching haphazardly to the sky, the ethereal colour of her face a reflection of the gum bark itself. Clasping the tree with both hands, she leaned her head briefly on its solid aromatic trunk, then swivelled dramatically around.

"This is the street, isn't it?" she demanded, more than queried.

"Yes," responded Joel casually. "It's changed a lot, hasn't it?" He shrugged and looked away.

Marcia was in no mood for small talk. Fury filled her face. "I can't believe you brought me here. You haven't got a clue, have you?"

"What do you mean, Marcia?" he asked gently, as he stroked her face, trying to calm her.

She shoved him away. "How dare you bring me here."

"Why not? It's a beautiful street. Some of our best eating places are here."

"And is...?" Her voice trailed away, as tears shot into her eyes. She fought them away. She preferred Joel to see her coolly raging rather than womanly upset.

"Is what, Marcy?"

"I told you to stop calling me that."

"Get real, my dear. The name slips out easily. I don't mean to offend you. It's how I think of you, in my heart of hearts." He stood close by, wanting to comfort her, but seeing she was in no mood to be consoled, well, not by him anyway. "What did you want to know?"

Joel watched this beautiful woman stand in front of him, her face the same deathly, pale colour of the ghost gum she leaned back on, drawing solace from its solidity rather than from his. He watched her face intently as she tried to force the words out, and every time she tried, she gulped, fighting the tears that sprung into her eyes. He moved closer to wrap his arms around the tree, enclosing her in his comfort, but she shoved him aside. Hurt, he took a step back, and watched her gather courage to ask what she needed to ask.

"Is it still here?" Marcia asked distractedly, wringing her hands together, like a crazed woman.

Either Joel was being deliberately stubborn, or he truly was innocent to the question. "Is what still here?"

"You know," and Marcia stepped toward him, again nervously pounding his chest, oblivious to the passers-by who were starting to look at them strangely.

Joel noticed them and tried to steer her on, but she twisted away, and started to run back toward the car. He caught up to her quickly and grabbed her. In a voice that was more severe than she ever remembered hearing, he said, "get a grip on yourself woman. What the hell are you asking me? And why do you have to attack me every time you get upset? Here in the street, in this street, why do you have to embarrass me like this?"

"I don't care what I'm doing to you."

"No, you wouldn't, would you? Life has always been sweet for you. Not a care in the world."

"Don't give me that nonsense. How can you say that, particularly here in this street?"

"Don't you give me that line, particularly here in this street," Joel responded aggressively, "don't you forget that this street affects me too."

"Then why in the name of heaven did you bring us here?"

"Because we need to talk about what we share, and clearly, obviously, this street brings our common experiences back to us both. But remember that Marcia, it brings it back to both of us. You are not unique in the tough memories this street evokes."

"Perhaps we needed to talk before we came here."

"Hell Marcia, I've been trying to. But you wouldn't talk, remember?"

Marcia had no decent reply to this, he was right. She hated herself for doing so, but she burst out howling like a little girl. Joel instinctively moved to comfort her, but with a hand on his chest, she thrust him an arm's distance away. Her icy interior froze around her. She was caught inside a massive iceberg that nothing could melt.

"Take me home, Joel Trucker."

"But you haven't eaten all day."

"I'll eat something at home."

Without a word, Joel led her back to the tiny car, opened the passenger door for her, and drove off almost recklessly, certainly at speed. Marcia glanced irritably at him but didn't reproach him.

When they got to Marcia's apartment, Marcia made sure she was the first to speak. "I can't believe you're so cold and thoughtless toward me that you would take me back to that street."

"Cold?" Joel laughed a horrible cackle of disbelief, unlike his usual warm chuckle. "You accuse me of coldness when you are the Ice Maiden. You are the Princess of Ice, the Queen of the Snow,

Doctor Marcia Ice Maiden Newton, Collins, Knight. I don't know what it will take to melt you. We wouldn't be in this damn childish situation now if you'd talked to me years ago, instead of wrapping icicles around you, and refusing to let anyone with warmth come near to melt you." He glared at her.

"Are you finished?"

"Not really. There's much more I'd like to say."

"Well, I don't want to hear it," she responded haughtily, ever the frosty woman he accused her of being.

Joel couldn't stay angry for long, it was foreign to his personality. "Marcia, we've been through so much, most of it together, some of it alone. We work together now. This not talking properly presents a ridiculous situation."

"Only as ridiculous as you want it to be. We work together admirably because we are well-trained professionals who are superb at our jobs, but I don't want you ever to contact me again socially."

He shrugged nonchalantly. "Okay, I'll see you at your dad's house then," Joel replied triumphantly, with his usual grin on his handsome face.

"We can work out a schedule when you go and when I go."

Joel roared with laughter. "No way, sweetheart. You might bring rules and regulations into your play life, but I never will. Medicine is demanding enough with its precise techniques and strict procedures to follow. My social life is full of spontaneity, enjoyment, and liberated fun."

"Then go and play with someone else." Inside, she didn't mean this at all. She wanted to play with him with a desperation she had never known was possible.

Joel intuited this as well. "You will be a lonely, old maid Marcia. If you're not careful, you'll have no one to play with."

"That's my business," and huffily, without farewelling him, she stormed off.

Again, she lay on her bed and cried herself to sleep. She'd eaten nothing all day. On Sunday morning, she awoke in incredulity as she looked at her body. Again, she'd fallen asleep with her clothes on, for two nights in a row. What was happening to her?

How could that infuriatingly handsome man upset her equilibrium so profoundly? He was totally charming, very kind, naturally humorous, and great fun to be with. She wanted to play with him. Besides, he was such a warm sensual being, what woman wouldn't want to be with him? Why did he have to spoil everything and take her down the street she never wanted to go down again? Never again.

A little internal voice reminded her that he too had sound reason to find that street particularly difficult to walk down. Then why had he taken her there? What was the sense in that?

Marcia whimpered into her pillow. She had thought that she'd been away long enough to be able to cope with her tough memories of the place that still haunted her. But in all honesty, she wasn't coping with the past trauma. Marcia was not a woman to cope easily with the notion that she wasn't surviving competently. Her professional identity required her to believe that she was first-rate in all her dealings. In control of all aspects of life.

Vowing to concentrate on what she excelled in, namely her hospital work, she set out to have a relaxing day, to rebuild her strength for the following week. She turned her mobile phone off and ignored the persistent knock on the door that she presumed was her kindly neighbour.

Pouring lavender aromatherapy oil into her luxury spa bath, she turned up the bubble jets, put a favourite classical CD on, and was just about to plunge in when she gulped, she was starving. A plate of warmed croissants and some fresh fruit later, surrounded by sensual aromas and soothing bubbles, and she felt more herself.

In the afternoon, she lay about on the sofa dressed in a red silk kimono and read a new romantic novel. It kept her engrossed, she couldn't wait to see if the man would ever declare his love for the heroine, but the woman seemed to be playing hard to get. Why was she doing this?

She was still hungry, so she made herself an omelette with a side salad, and went to bed early to finish the novel.

The story ended happily, and Marcia drifted off into sleep wondering if love and real happiness would ever come her way. Her father's talk off destiny was haunting her. What was her destiny? Would she ever find love? Could she find a playmate? Was she really an Ice Maiden? Surely not. Well, maybe at times. What would it take for her to melt?

7

Marcia awoke feeling refreshed. This was a week for sheer profession-alism. She deliberately chose an austere, high necked, short-sleeved grey dress that flattered her figure, but was in no way provocative. Thankful for inheriting her mother's flawless complexion, she wore no make-up except for her trademark red lipstick.

Steeling herself in preparation for seeing the little, old, white, Volkswagen parked beside her glossy, red, sports car, and more im-portantly, seeing the little car's big owner, she braced herself for yet another vocationally fulfilling, but socially alienating week. Again, as nature, fate, or the gods, or perhaps all three were willing them together, they arrived at the hospital car park at the same time. How did he do that? Did he wait around the corner until she arrived? Surely not.

Una was in the car with Joel, and she called out warmly to Marcia. Marcia noticed how lovely she looked this morning, her hair an enviable cascade of impressive curls. In fact, she looked radiant, as if she and Joel had had a wonderful Sunday together. Why shouldn't they enjoy the weekend? As Joel had told Marcia, there was no way he was going to sit about mooching, waiting for life and love to happen to him. No, he'd create a rich life and enjoy as much of it as possible. He was a man with passion and sensuality flowing through his veins. He wasn't a man to deprive himself of fleshly delights.

An empty hollowness threatened to engulf Marcia, and she swallowed hard to avoid tears rushing to her eyes. Self-pity wouldn't do. She threw a curt, ridiculously formal "good morning, Doctor Trucker, good morning, Nurse Una," over her shoulders, knowing that Joel would hate her abrupt, prim coldness. Was she really an Ice Maiden? She could see why he had called her that. Briefcase in hand, she marched into the hospital briskly, alone. Was she destined to always be alone?

The next weeks passed uneventfully. Both doctors performed their respective tasks admirably, as the accomplished medical professionals they both were. Joel waited until she scrubbed up before he entered the preparation room, addressed her in theatre only in terms of the patient's immediate needs or concerns, and avoided her afterwards. Morning tea was rare, and lunch was in snatched moments, always taken as part of a group, even though the nature of the group varied daily, and the old friends sat as far away from each other as possible. Despite the distance, they could still feel each other's presence.

In the washrooms after surgery, they went about their showers and changing without a single word spoken personally to each other. Usually, other medical staff were using the facilities. There was little chatter. In the afternoon ward rounds, they went their separate ways, Joel to check his patients' progress, she to reassure new patients that all will be well on the next day's operations. Joel no longer waited for Marcia at the exit, as he had done daily in the first week. She missed the ritual. She pined for his attention.

On the first Monday after the eventful weekend, Marcia had gone to her father's house straight after work, and taken him out for dinner, making sure that she would not accidentally bump into Joel's house visit again. She explained carefully to her father that she wanted to see him, and she certainly wanted to use his swimming pool, but she did not want to see Joel there. Her father couldn't understand her and started to probe, but Marcia refused to be forthcoming. She saw the acute sadness in his face but thrust his hurt aside. She felt that there was no other choice. She kept wondering if she was an Ice Maiden. Now Joel had placed this image in her mind, she couldn't get it out of her head.

Reluctantly, her father agreed to let her know when Joel was coming around. He'd acquired the latest iPhone and was proud of his new skills in texting. He reminded her that, as had been his practice since boyhood, Joel appreciated the way he was welcomed, and Bill was glad of his companionship, and that he often called around uninvited. Marcia knew that in telling her this, he was reproaching her gently for not contacting him as much as she should do, and clearly, not as often as Joel obviously still did. What a good man!

Her father expressed his deep concern at his only child's isolationist tendencies, and the only way to console him was to agree that she would start to contact some of her previous acquaintances.

Her father's final comment to her she drove her sleek Jaguar up his steep drive was, "I don't know why you're avoiding Joel, my dear child. I'm sure you must have your reasons, but he is such an incredibly decent man. You know that he is like a son to me, I always presumed that one day, he would become my son-in-law. He has always loved you."

"No dad," she answered dogmatically, "you and mum, and Myra and Sam, always wanted us together, so you presumed that love was in the air."

"It is, my dear."

"No dad, he has a gorgeous Irish nurse beside him every day and presumably night."

"For someone as intelligent as you Marcia, you're extraordinarily naive at times."

This wasn't the way her father ever talked with her. She drove off disturbed, not at all sure what he was implying. However, she took his advice, and decided to look up some of her past acquaintances. This was not going to be easy, not after all that she had been through, and her total avoidance of them over these past years. How could she just bounce back into their lives? Would they even be interested in her?

She wasn't the dynamic companion like Joel. Joel! His name, his image, memories of his touch constantly hovered somewhere in her thoughts. She was relieved to have at least an idea of what some of their friends were doing, thanks to the conversation she'd already had on the beach with Joel.

Suddenly, she felt like she was a totally, silly novice at something as straightforward and simple to most people, as contacting old friends. Presumably, most people simply picked up a mobile phone, then called, emailed, or texted, and introduced themselves again, apologised briefly for the silence over these years, laughed about it, and made plans to meet. Was it this easy? Could it be this simple? If so, why was she feeling so muddled?

She hadn't even kept up-to-date with mobile phone changes and didn't want to join Facebook. Reluctantly, she accepted she might have to, to find people's names. Even doing this felt strange. She entered the most basic, minimalist profile. She did not intend posting much, she was using Facebook simply to find old friends. She found an old photo that half obscured her face as her profile picture. Even if you looked closely, you couldn't be entirely sure it was her. Partial anonymity suited her aloofness.

Nothing seemed simple to Marcia, except for work. That was what she did best. That was what she had thrown her life into: study, books, tests, exams; then work, work, work, more reading to keep abreast of changing trends, seminars to attend, and conferences to give papers at and discuss advances in paediatric anaesthesia. All this work she could do. She didn't need a man to help her.

She loved work and being part of the hustle and bustle of the big hospital, where everyone paid such a vital part in keeping the institution alive and dynamic. Yet for the first time in her life, she had wistfully begun to watch the patients' families and friends as they empathised with the pain and the suffering of their sick children, and then showed such intense loving care as their dear ones gained strength. There were lots of hugs and kisses in the children's wards.

Aware that her own biological clock was ticking away, she'd begun to wonder about what it might be like to have a child of her own, rather than always caring for someone else's child. These were foreign thoughts to her consciousness, almost outrageous to her, and certainly most unwelcome, because along with them, always came a vision of a tall man with broad shoulders, wonderfully curly hair, and with the deepest, liveliest, darkest eyes that still met hers over their surgical masks.

He certainly was a lion, King of the hospital wards, King of the jungle of her emotions. Once, she had stood at the door of a hospital room and he hadn't looked up. He was cradling a newborn baby he had done emergency surgery on. She was only ten days old. He had saved her life. He was gentle and abundantly tender with her. The parents looked on adoringly, and Marcia walked on, unnoticed, but deeply affected by his warm compassion.

Marcia's thoughts meandered back to her current task. She might not be good at her emotions, but she was an expert at accomplishing set tasks. Getting a piece of paper, she scribbled the names of all the friends she remembered who she particularly liked. She deliberately crossed out all the men and women who Joel said had recently had a child. This wasn't a world she wanted to enter. Not now. She checked the women's names and crossed them off when she couldn't find them on Facebook. She guessed that some had married and taken on their husband's surname.

In shock, she looked down at the list. There were two women's names and three men's names left. How pathetic! She rang the first woman's number, only to get an answering machine that said that Selena was away in the Himalayas, trekking, but messages could be left with her housemate. She knew the next woman on the list Jo-Belle, was a promiscuous lesbian, and while she was great fun to be with, Marcia felt unable to cope with anything complicated, so crossed her name off. Any excuse.

That left the three men. She never liked one of them much, he was dominating and bullishly argumentative, so she scrubbed his name off.

Feeling very nervous, she rang the phone number of one of the men, and when a young woman answered, she felt too shy to speak and so she quickly hung up. This was not typical behaviour for her.

That left only one man's name, Clive Burns. From all their past friends, she'd been left with one name, how wretchedly sad was that? From what she could remember, Clive was a quiet, unassuming, pleasant man who taught in a local primary school.

Tentatively, she phoned him, and was encouraged when he genuinely sounded excited to hear from her. She was relieved that he asked questions of her without prying unnecessarily, and she was grateful when he suggested they meet for dinner.

Preparing for this occasion threw Marcia into a spin. She rarely read women's fashion magazines, so she had no idea of helpful tips. She didn't have a sister to borrow clothes from. She had no close women friends to phone for advice. Her mother was dead. What a sad woman she was.

Previously working in tropical Australian heat, she was accustomed to wearing khaki shorts and cotton sleeveless shirts, with the occasional short skirt and tee-shirt. Clothes from the last five years were dated and overly casual. She'd sweated in many of them and dumped them in a charity box.

On her return to Sydney, she had bought classic work dresses and conservative suits, but her wardrobe for social occasions needed serious updating. Money wasn't a problem, it never had been. The incentive to please, impress, and be seductive had long been absent. Did she want to seduce Clive? Definitely not. She had no idea what he was like now. People change. She'd changed. These confused intentions threw her into a further whirl. This was meeting up with an old friend, nothing less, but nothing more. She didn't have to elevate it to the status of a date. That would make her feel nervous.

Needing some after work distractions to what she now accepted was a very lonely life, she treated herself to the most extensive shopping spree she had undertaken since her mother was alive.

Cleverly, she asked the experienced shop assistants for advice with each new outfit, getting them to suggest accessories, shoes, scarves, and jewellery to match.

Doing so brought back memories of going to beauty parlours with her mother, so she reinstated the weekly facials that once, in her past, she had religiously enjoyed with her mother, and disbanded when work took top priority. It felt good to have some pampering. Safe hands on her skin.

The night of the dinner with Clive, she didn't equivocate what to wear. She chose a simple, straight, black dress, in slinky twenties style. She wore a conservative, but neat grey jacket over the dress, covering her top. They had agreed to meet at a particular restaurant, and she sat waiting, wondering if this was a date or a polite dinner with two old acquaintances. It had to be the latter. There was only one man she craved a date with, but she kept sending wrong messages to him. What a fool. And Una, what role did she play in Joel's life? She really wasn't sure.

Clive was a few minutes late, but as soon as she saw him, she decided this was not a date. She could never fall for a man who was so unfashionable looking, and going grey so young, but then she felt horrible for prejudging him simply by his appearance. He was kind, thoughtful, and overeager to see her. Several times in his enthusiasm to pour her wine, he spilled a few drops, helplessly clumsy with his chubby fingers, but wanting to please.

In fact, it was so easy to please Clive, that he was overjoyed when she pecked him goodnight on the cheek and agreed to meet again. She was desperate for uncomplicated friendship.

They met again. Despite Marcia's request for Clive to organise social gatherings with some of their past mutual acquaintances, he did not. His excuse was that he was too busy at school, particularly now with the pantomime that he was directing fast approaching. He was severely stressed out that the pupil's mother who had agreed to be Cinderella, had broken her ankle, and none of the female teachers would agree to act as a substitute.

As a laugh, and because she was lonely, Marcia told him that she had been part of a drama group at university, and she agreed to play the part. From that moment, she spent many evenings in his boring little house over hastily prepared microwave suppers, learning her lines. They were hardly difficult, it wasn't like she was studying for her medical exams, they had been truly tough, incredibly challenging. These evenings were a welcome break from the demands of hospital life, and it was nice to leave work to go and meet with someone. At least Clive's company was amusing, casual, and she was propelled into a different world.

The first practice at the school was a sheer joy. The children were delighted that they had such a beautiful main character in their play, and they giggled when the teacher, Mr Burns, introduced her as Dr Cinderella Knight. She hadn't acted since university days, and before that, in her high school days, and she accepted that now, the drama was a form of therapy for her, as she danced gleefully across the school stage along with the excited school children. Their energy rubbed off, and she felt herself giggling with them. It was fun, and there wasn't much entertainment in her life.

Afterwards, she shared a cup of tea and a plain biscuit with Clive in the staff room and returned home. It was an effortless, unfussy friendship. Was it enough?

8

Marcia had completed the first month in hospital. She waited on the last Friday of the month to see the new roster go up for the next month's team. She stood emotionless as she read her name, along with Una Byrne, Doctor Joel Trucker, and a mixture of names she did and did not know. The team had not changed much. Engrossed in reading, she stepped back on someone's foot.

"Still squashing me, are you Doctor Knight?" came a quiet, but deep voice, and Marcia's heart unintentionally raced a little quicker. Why did he do that to her? Every time she was close to him, she felt his presence as if he was embracing her.

"Sorry, Doctor Trucker."

A steadying hand came up to her arm as Joel stood back, taking in the beauty in front of him. Marcia wore a sapphire blue, sleeveless, long jumpsuit. It was something different for her to wear. She'd never worn a jumpsuit before, the shop assistant had persuaded her that it suited her beautifully. Her startling blue eyes reflected the colour of her new clothes. Joel noticed Marcia look away, and then look quickly back at him.

"You have looked much happier lately, Marcia. I'm very pleased to see this." He seemed genuine. When she didn't reply, he went on.

"I hope this doesn't mean you have met some wonderful man who has swept you off your feet." His eyes twinkled in jest.

"Well actually, I'm seeing Clive Burns."

She may as well have said that she was seeing a gorilla, or James Bond, or Superman. "Clive Burns?" Joel asked in disgusted disbelief. His smile vanished in an instant.

"Yes, is there something wrong with that?" She was very defensive.

"No, not if you don't mind being bored senseless."

Oversensitively, she said, "I'm not bored, I'm playing Cinderella in the school play."

With this remark, Joel cracked into hysterical, uncontrollable laughter, calling out, "Cinderella, Cinderella, come to the ball," gripping his sides to try to gain some composure.

Marcia despised public humiliation, and other staff were crowding around the noticeboard to check rosters. She tried to make an unobtrusive escape, but it was not possible.

A young, particularly lively nurse who was constantly trying to flirt with Joel, sidled up to him, and seductively said, "I'll be your Cinderella, take me to the ball."

"Go lose your slipper elsewhere, my dear," he responded patronisingly, but the group's interests had been caught. As with a Chinese whisper, where one tiny comment can flow around the room and return in a totally different format, the questions poured out.

"Who's Cinderella?"

"Who's lost a slipper?"

"What slipper?"

"This ball or some other ball?"

"Who's taking you to the ball?"

"Did I never tell you? You won't believe me."

"Which Cinderella?"

"Which ball?"

"Are we having a pantomime, after all?"

Joel played the questions like a ringmaster at a circus, taking each question seriously, but then teasing each person with wickedly ridiculous answers. Marcia watched from a distance, quietly admiring his abundant self-confidence, and the way he used humour to relax everyone. She was grateful to him for deflecting the attention away from her. Everyone except Marcia were in spirited frames after this hilarity.

Seeing her bewildered face, Una saw a gap in the crowd, and pushed through colleagues to reach her. "Who are you going to the ball with?" she asked.

Marcia could not believe it. Una, the woman who spent so much time with the man who with a mere glance her way, wielded the power to disturb her emotions, was mocking her community-minded contribution to the school children's Christmas pageant.

"Well," she responded harshly, "with a school kid actually."

"A school pupil? Marcia, if you don't mind me asking, what are you talking about?"

Marcia shrugged and moved off in humiliated haste, only to see Una and Joel in a comradely huddle, conversing and giggling together.

Una came racing back to her. "Now I understand Dr Knight. I'm so sorry for getting it wrong, Joel has explained it to me. I hadn't realised you are a real live Cinderella in a school play. That's wonderful."

"That's okay Una," and she went charging down the corridor, anxious to rid herself of the presence of this auburn beauty who she saw as such a threat. But a threat to what? How could she lust after a man with whom she became so readily frustrated with?

Una was stubbornly persistent. She hated misunderstandings with anyone, let alone an important colleague. She came after Marcia again. "Dr Knight, who are you going to the ball with?"

Impatiently, she responded, "I've told you already Una, a school boy."

"No Marcia, the hospital ball."

"What ball?"

Una grinned. "I don't believe you. It's the talk of everyone, who's going with who, and who's wearing what."

Marcia only now noticed that Joel had been observing this conversation with amusement on his face. He walked across to them. "Grab your gear, Una my dear," he said as he playfully tossed her auburn curls over her shoulders, "I'll meet you by the car." Doing precisely as she was told, Una trotted off.

"King of the Jungle aye, Dr Trucker?"

"That's nothing compared to being Cinderella, pride of the ball."

"Are you mocking me?"

"Oh, lighten up Marcia. Have you forgotten how to smile?" Joel reached out to touch her hair, but this meant little to her, she'd just seen him do this to Una too, so it was a meaningless gesture. It wasn't something he was doing especially to her. It was simply a flirtatious response to any pretty woman. She stepped back. He persisted. "Marcia, can I see you this weekend?"

The response was instant. "No." How desperately she wanted to scream, "yes, yes, please Joel, please come around and hold me tight and let me hold you and never let you go. Clive might be companionable, but he does nothing for me passionately." Instead, she reiterated her rejection, "no."

"Then can I ask you an innocent question?"

"Is that possible?"

"How come you manage to avoid me at your father's house? I know you've been there. I can smell your perfume lingering. I'd recognise it anywhere. Why are you never there when I'm there?"

She smirked cruelly. "Ask my dad."

"I have, many times, and he just shrugs. He's not himself these days, he seems coy, uncomfortably so, which is not like him. Usually, he's so honest and straightforward. It's as if he's miserable about something."

Gloating, Marcia retorted, "I never go straight after work like I know you do occasionally. I get him to tell me your pattern, and he phones or texts me when you arrive."

"So, that's where he disappears to every time I arrive. That's just plain sad, Marcia. I can't believe it. That's devious. You're distorting his natural honesty. Also, importantly, you're depriving him of our joint company, and you know how much he craves that."

"And," she smirked unkindly, ignoring his chastisement, "Sometimes I drive past and if I see your old car sitting there, I drive on."

"So," he responded in a flash, "if I disrupt my pattern, get Bill in the pool with me the moment I arrive, not giving him the chance to grab his phone, or I leave my car parked a block away, we should occasionally coincide."

Marcia suddenly couldn't believe how silly she'd been in telling him her actions to avoid him, and how quick he'd been in response. He was like that. Speedy to his target. King of the jungle. She glared at him grinning at her. "Clever fellow, aren't you?"

"Marcia, how about agreeing to come around tonight?" He saw that she was sorely tempted, and his face warmed to the hope. "Your father misses us being there together. It was something he'd been looking forward to with your return home. He tells me this every time I visit."

Disguising her disappointment, she said, "I can't."

"Why not?"

"I've a final dress rehearsal, and that's the truth, no excuses needed."

"Cinderella?"

"Yes."

"Then, dinner with the bore?"

'Clive's alright."

"Yeah, for a boring old sod." Joel's disappointment was so markedly evident that she was touched. Una came skipping out of the hospital.

"See you next week Joel," Marcia called out quietly, mentally undressing him and blushing as he came across to her as she bent over to pack her briefcase, and a long slender leg was exposed.

"Red lacy ones, Marcia."

"You're only guessing that I'd wear ones that match my dress."

"You always used to, but you are wrong this time. I saw them as you bent over. They're red lace." For the first time for ages, she laughed spontaneously with him. It felt good. Natural. Heart-warming.

"Correct."

He grasped this moment to take her hand and she tingled all down her spine as she felt his warm, safe, surgeon's hand clasp her clammy fingers. He talked intensely and rapidly. "Marcia, I've found these last weeks unbelievably difficult. You asked me to give you space and not contact you socially. I'm respecting your wishes, and I haven't rung you, or called, or pressured you at work. I also respected your request that we treat each other at work purely professionally, and I've tried to do so, but oh my God, what I've done with you while you were in the shower each day, you'd never dream of it."

Marcia broke her hand free, and happily asked, "what do you mean? What have you done?" There was a faint, curious smile on her face.

"That would be telling, wouldn't it? Settle it babes. I've ripped your clothes off in my mind, all in my imagination of course, the fantasy world of one lonely, lovesick doctor."

"Lonely, what about Una?"

"Get a life Marcia." She had no idea what he meant. Was she totally unworldly? "Marcia, I thought I could cope with the restrictions you placed on me, because I expected to see you a lot at Bill's, but instead, you're off gallivanting with some boring, old deadhead of a schoolteacher."

"He's not such a bore," said Marcia, stoically defending him, not sure why she was doing so. He was a bore, a mind-numbing bore. It was the youngsters who kept her alive, not him.

"Well, he must be teaching you some tricks. Perhaps you're teaching him some. You certainly have looked stunning these past weeks." He suddenly became serious. "Marcia, would you be my Cinderella?"

"What do you mean?"

"Marcia, sometimes I don't know what planet you live on. As I heard Una tell you, the Christmas ball is a hospital institution. Everyone goes to it, and I mean everyone. The women look forward to it for weeks. How can you have missed the talk?"

"You're right, I guess I live on another hemisphere." She looked despondent.

"Or you choose to cut yourself off from all that's sensual, spontaneous, and sexy for that matter."

"Not always."

"I'm glad to hear it. Marcia, would you come to the ball with me?"

"What about Una?"

"What about Una? I'm not always her Prince Charming." What on earth did this mean? That he liked two women at once? Really? It seemed impossible to believe. If it was true, did that make him fickle or what? Did he no longer value faithfulness? He used to. She gulped as the questions rushed at her.

"When is it?"

"I can't believe you don't know. There are posters stuck up all over the hospital staff rooms. It's always held on the second last Saturday before Christmas."

"I can't go then. That's the finale of the pantomime."

"It can't be." He looked crestfallen.

"It is."

"When does the pantomime finish? It can't be too late if it's a school function." He was determined to be proactive. Problems were there to be solved.

"It should finish at about nine o'clock, then there's a party for the cast."

"Do your play, and I'll pick you up straight away, take you home, and you can change in a hurry. In fact, I'll come and watch you."

"You can't do that," she said, mortified at the idea.

"Look, we'll sort out the mechanics later, please say yes."

"It wouldn't give me time to prepare."

"The ball goes late, it certainly goes on until the early hours of the next morning. Many people must come late, especially those who have been on late hospital shifts. I can pick you up, and even let you have a glass of cordial with the children, whisk you back to your apartment, and we can be there at the ball by after ten."

"I suppose," she said doubtfully, wondering how on earth she'd get glammed up with such speed.

Never one to be dismayed for long, he sarcastically responded, "that's the most enthusiastic acceptance I've had for years. I look forward to it."

"Sorry, I always let you down."

"You never let me down Marcia," he swooped in and kissed her quickly on the cheek before she had a chance to object. She came alive with his touch.

She was going to two balls on one night. Would Joel be her Prince Charming?

9

Marcia drove straight off for her final dress rehearsal. She knew that Joel was right, Clive was a bore, but a companionable one at that, and that was easy to manage for now.

Her face burned with the passion of Joel's kiss, a man whose blood flowed with heat. There was nothing boring about him. Why then could she not yield to his heart's desires? Hers too, if she was honest. But honesty hadn't been her friend for so long now that she'd forgotten what she was like. She went through the motions of life, pretence coming easily. She glanced at her mouth in the mirror, expecting them to be blood red. They were. It was her lipstick, her trademark.

She shuddered at the thought of spending the evening with Clive. Perhaps she might excuse herself early on the pretext of needing to see her father. But she had told Joel that she wasn't going to be there. Would he change his plans? Would he visit Bill so that he wouldn't be lonely, or would he not visit, knowing there was no chance of bumping into Marcia? Why did life feel so confusing?

She admitted how hungry she felt to see Joel out of work time, to have some of his hot passion flow through her, melt her icicles, her cold, barrier that she had built to keep herself protected. Could one kiss do this? Yes, it seemed so. There were droplets around her, perhaps her iceberg was melting, just a bit.

She drove to Clive's school with a heavy heart. This wasn't what she wanted to do tonight, or tomorrow, or the day after. She sat in the car for a while, getting her headspace into the right place. When it was in a better space, she stepped out, thinking only of the children. They were great fun and always lifted her mood, excited to share the stage with her.

Marcia admitted how much she was enjoying the fun of the pantomime. It was light relief after the intense concentration needed of being in the surgical theatre. The sheer joy of watching the children's delight relaxed her oppressed spirits. She waved casually to Clive, then joined the youngsters in the girls' dressing rooms.

The pupils loved dressing up in their costumes, they adored being made-up by their teachers and volunteer mothers, then they were diligent in remembering their lines on stage. They kept whispering them as they clambered into their costumes. Marcia entered the spirit of the occasion, and laughed when the children giggled, mimicking their shrieks of delight in anticipation of performing before a crowd. She too jumped up and down on the spot, anxious to get on with the production. This was like much-needed therapy to her troubled soul. Drama-in-motion.

When Marcia pulled out her gown, the girls drooled. It was an old wedding dress that she had bought in a second-hand shop. As she stood there and started to dramatise her role, dressed in her tatty old outfit, pretending to sweep the floor, the children could hardly wait to see her transformed into what seemed to them, a stunning ball gown. She was their princess, a special, Doctor Princess. Marcia smiled at their enthusiastic exhilaration. She wished she could share it fully.

Tonight, she was totally play-acting, pretending that she was engrossed in the play as they were, but her heart was elsewhere, it was in full fantasy flight, flying toward one handsome doctor. He set her heart racing, making her body come alive. He made her icy exterior melt, made her feel warm and fuzzy inside. Why couldn't she show this warmth? Why did her icy exterior remain rigid? She soared in the heavens at the mere thought of being close to him.

Instead of the stage in front of her, she could see in her mind's eye Joel lying on the deck chair beside her father. She imagined that Bill would be dressed in comfy shorts and an oversized tropical patterned shirt, his Aussie Akubra hat plonked on his head, even though the sun had dropped low in the sky.

Joel would probably have only his bathers on, his glorious body glistening with drops of moisture that she'd love to lick off. Now. He'd shove one hand sensuously through his dark curls, the other hand would rest on his muscular thigh. Above his thigh, deep in the pocket of his brief, speedo bathers, how would he look there? Marcia could well imagine and felt longing. This was not the place for this desire to be happening.

But Marcia came alive at the masculine vision that was forming in her mind. She felt loose and sensual for once, as she ran her hands slowly over the muddy brown, deliberately torn, cloth apron that covered her costume. Despite its roughness, she felt her skin scream-ing to be touched by masculine hands, hands other than her own.

She wanted to yell at the top of her voice, "Joel, where are you? Come and touch me, everywhere. Now." He wasn't there to listen to her silent cry. She craved his presence with a desperate longing.

Instead, she heard a demanding voice that she had begun to despise. Its whining tone annoyed her. "Cinderella, are you ready?" Clive stood there, as if he had cracked a funny joke, but she could see that he was flustered as the cries of the children were tittering about them.

Marcia was mortified. She'd been stroking her body. How much had he observed? Did he see anything? No matter, she didn't care what he saw. He meant little to her, although she suspected that he did not understand this indifference properly. She had started to see the semi-lustful look in his eyes, making her squirm in embarrassment. She must let him know soon, it wasn't fair to lead him on. She didn't care to pursue her friendship to anything romantic. Not that she had been leading him on, but perhaps his ideas were different to hers. The friendship was feeling flat, like it was not something she wanted anymore.

Joel was right. He often was. He usually was. Clive was one big boring sod. She felt no attraction toward him. In fact, she was starting to be repulsed by his presence. She was no longer even enjoying being in his company. To be truthful, she hadn't ever really liked his company. She'd rather be by herself. It was less complicated.

Tonight, the play ran smoothly, with only a few minor hiccups that could be easily rectified. The drama teacher working with Clive was very encouraging and helpful to the children, providing useful advice to improve their next performance.

The children were awestruck at the vision of Marcia transformed into a beautiful Princess, dancing with Prince Charming, now school-teacher Mr Clive Burns. Marcia had groaned when she heard that the schoolboy who was to play the prince lost his nerve once he saw Marcia transformed from her tatty servant garments into her white satin elegance, as if she was a princess in real life.

After the play ended, there was little privacy in the girl's changing rooms as Marcia climbed out of the second-hand wedding dress, the girls' eyes dropping demurely. As she did so, she became very thoughtful.

She wondered about the woman who had worn the dress. Who was she? How old was she when she wore it? Where was she now? Was her wedding day the happiest day of her life? Wasn't that what childish myths were about. Why had she dumped the dress in a charity store? Or had she given it away to an aid organisation to help others? Did she want to be rid of it, and with it, discard old, faded, memories? Was she still married? Was she miserable? So many curious, interesting, unanswered questions.

Or might the bride have been deliriously happy, and want to pass on a little of her happiness in the form of her dress? It was a simple dress. Perhaps some women had modest aspirations and could be happy easily.

Marcia wondered about wearing a wedding gown. What would it be like? It might be simple in style, but it would be elaborately beaded, tightly fitting, elegant, stunning, a dress her mother would have helped her to purchase. No mother. No wedding dress. No prospects. Marcia sighed deeply, a sigh of frustrated desire.

Marcia could see the girls' eyes alternately gazing in wonder at her, then dropping them shyly when they caught her eye. Marcia knew how far a smile went with children, so she kept smiling. It was a relief to know that she excelled in this one simple task of making children happy. There was nothing complicated about this.

Inside, she was not smiling. That rotter Clive Burns had taken unappreciated liberties with his sudden elevation to Prince Charming. On stage, he had held her tighter than he needed to, closer than he should have, and once, he had rubbed his prickly face against hers, so close that she could smell his foul breath. Ooh, she groaned inside at the thought.

There was only one man's arms she wanted around her, one handsome doctor who occupied her waking thoughts, every second when she wasn't working. That was part of why she was such a hard worker. Constant demanding work was a distraction, not letting her give in to her desires.

Tonight's stage liberties decided it, for good. As soon as the right moment came, she would tell Clive that she was tired and needed to make her escape, for good. This prince was certainly not her Prince

Charming. That man was elsewhere. She'd lose her glass slipper for Doctor Joel Trucker any day.

Her mind sailed back to him. Perhaps when Joel found out that she wasn't going to be at her father's house, maybe he'd gone elsewhere. Perhaps at this precise moment, he was wrapped around the gorgeous Una Byrne. If it was spontaneity and fun that he wanted, Una could give it to him in abundance, holding nothing back, she was quite sure of that. Her wild, wonderful laughter could be heard almost a ward away. Everyone adored her happy, outgoing personality, children, and adults alike.

Marcia gathered her personal items into her bag and headed toward Clive who was surrounded by a group of concerned parents who wanted further, clarifying details about the final performances. Ignoring them, he hurried over to her and put a clumsy, hairy paw on her shoulders, and furtively whispered in her ear, "wasn't that lovely to be crushed together on the dance floor. You and me," and he winked knowingly.

Marcia pulled away disgusted. "I don't think so, Clive."

Clive looked like a disappointed schoolboy who hadn't made the A-grade football team. "But I thought after the party next week, you and I could, you know what," and again he winked conspiratorially.

Marcia shivered inside and shuddered visibly. "I won't be at the party Clive. I'll do the final performance as I promised, but then I have to leave promptly."

"But I was looking forward to the after's."

"The after's?" she asked in amazed disbelief, screwing up every feature on her face, her eyes and mouth stretched in a repulsed grimace. "Am I an after-dinner mint? I have no idea what you mean."

"You know," he kept winking childishly, "you and I are a couple now, aren't we, I thought it was about time we did it."

"Did it?" asked Marcia in bemused shock. "You mean, have sex?"

He swooped in and grabbed her arm. "Sh, we're surrounded

by school children. You can't mention that word here." He was completely flustered, and looked most unattractive with his face screwed up and his arms flapping about.

"Clive, you really have misinterpreted our friendship. I thought you understood exactly where we stand. I sought you out as a past friend, for a bit of companionship, that's it, nothing more. I helped you out in this play for the fun of doing drama with children, that's it, no more. I'll see you at the productions, but no longer at your house. I couldn't trust you anymore."

He looked extremely pathetic as she turned back for a quick, last glance. He had a hangdog look as if he was a man robbed of a well-deserved prize. Her. How gross. He also looked podgy, unappealing, and old. She knew you shouldn't judge someone solely based on their looks, but tonight was a decider, she didn't want anything more to do with him. She watched him fuss over some pupils, like the fusspot he was, and wondered sympathetically why he lived such a lonely life. Surely, he could find someone he was compatible with. But then, who was she to talk? She lived a lonely life too.

Getting into her car, she sighed audibly. It was a relief to be away from his clawing presence, alone with her thoughts and desires for Doctor Joel Trucker. Peacefully alone.

Driving toward her father's house, Marcia felt a joyous skip in her heart as she thought of the possibility of seeing Joel. He had warned her how quickly she would bore with Clive, and he was right. She felt sickened at the thought of Clive's touch, even fumbling with her back bra-strap under the satin as he whirled her around the school stage.

Instead, she imagined what it might be like to have Joel's arms around her, whirling her around the dance floor, pulling her in tight, one arm around her waist, his face close to hers, his sweet breath on her neck. Oh, she longed for his touch and closeness. The ball wasn't far away. What a different Cinderella she would be.

10

Marcia sat quietly at the top of her father's drive for a few seconds. The old familiar Volkswagen wasn't there. Joel must be living it up with Una. She admitted to her disappointment.

Not wanting to let her father know her feelings, she burst into the house in an unusual, but welcome, light-hearted frame. Not once did he let her down, he was utterly delighted to see her, hugging her tightly. As he'd eaten already, she raided his refrigerator. He enjoyed gourmet cooking and always had a well-stocked pantry, packed full of nutritious and tasty ingredients. She quickly threw together a salad, throwing a diced, ripe avocado on the top.

They sat in the kitchen chatting easily about the week's operations and the different children's responses to surgery. Nothing stopped the flow of conversation until they heard the familiar chug of an old beetle car crawling up the drive. For two seconds, Marcia froze. The eyes of father and daughter locked across the well-worn, rustic, pine table.

With a loving, fatherly tone, Bill cautioned her. "Don't be too hard on yourself Marcia. Be open to all the possibilities that life throws in your direction."

"I don't know what you mean," she responded, stubbornness setting in her eyes.

"There is life and love to be grasped."

At this exact moment, Joel burst into the room, carrying an enormous watermelon on his shoulder. "Who's grasping the love of my life?" he joked, and put a quick kiss on Marcia's head, hugged the old man who was a second father to him, placed the watermelon on a chopping board, and cut it into slices, deftly flicking the pips away. Marcia could see his firm back muscles flexing and his arm muscles taut with the cutting motion. His body was magnificent. Even from the back view, she was excited merely watching him perform this simple domestic task.

The mere notion of performance sent sensual thrills shivering through her. This was quite different to the school performance she had come from.

Marcia sat munching the sweet, juicy melon, feeling as if this evening had been orchestrated. On the other hand, perhaps she was becoming paranoid. She was self-consciously aware, as both men had reminded her more than once, that Joel called in on Bill more frequently than she did. However, tonight, she sensed that they wanted jointly to say something. Please God, not the dreaded topic she avoided, she pleaded to the heavens. Joel's eyes were drawn to the arc in her neck as she gazed upward, just for a moment. Marcia lowered her eyes, they were drawn magnetically to his.

"So, why are you both quiet?" She broke the silence, trying to sound lighthearted.

The men looked at each other, each wanting the other person to start. Two strong affectionate men, one ageing but still a looker, the other young, virile, desirable, and bursting with potent power.

The older man began. "We are getting very close to Christmas Marcia, and yet, you've not mentioned it to us."

"There's no problem," she shrugged, "I've done most of my Christmas shopping."

"That's not what we mean Marcia. Joel has come home every year for Christmas, you haven't."

"So what?" She squirmed, uncertain if this was a mere statement or a rebuke. She was over-analysing everything these days. It was becoming tiring.

"Don't get irritable, my dear," and he placed a fatherly hand over hers.

Joel kept the conversation alive. "We'll be having Christmas here, as usual. Your dad kindly supplies most of the food, and mum and the extended family prepare it, and we all bring drinks to share."

"Yes, and?" Marcia looked about her for effect. "What's your point?"

"Are you going to be alright seeing people again, Marcia? You won't have seen the old Christmas crowd since..." Bill's voice trailed off, the unspoken hovering uninvited, and uncertain.

"Since she went away," Joel added diplomatically. He was a peace-maker. He'd be useful in the United Nations.

Marcia stood up, gripping the table so hard that her knuckles turned white. "Since the deaths you mean." She looked from her dad to Joel and back to the heavens. "Death, death, death, why doesn't anyone mention the forbidden D-word?"

"We do," answered Bill quickly and quietly, "Joel and I talk about it a lot, but we didn't know if you are ready to."

"I especially didn't, Marcia," added Joel, not at all afraid to speak frankly in front of Bill, given that he shared more personal details with him than with his own father or anyone else in the world. "I didn't know how to resume talking with you, not after your reaction to being in the notorious street the other night." He'd already shared the story with her father, who was deeply troubled when he heard of Marica's reactions.

"Well, I'll be okay on Christmas Day," she said more confidently than she felt. She wasn't about to voice her anxiety. She had been thinking about how hard it was going to be. Brighter than she felt, she said, "everyone will skirt politely around me, and ask all the obvious easy questions about being away, and coming back, and working now with Joel."

"Is that what you want Marcia? Do you want people to skirt around the truth?" Joel wanted to probe further, but held off pushing her, appreciating how delicate she was.

"I don't know what I want," lied Marcia, craving Joel's arms to go around her as they did once before, and hold her tight, and never let her go, while they shared all the details of their past.

Bill stood up suddenly. "I'm feeling a little weary tonight. I'm going to read for a while in my study, then go to bed. I'll leave you young ones to lock up for me," and he kissed his daughter good night. "Come again soon, love, you're welcome any time."

"Did you have that planned?" asked Marcia mysteriously, fully aware of the charisma of this young medical man over her.

"Oh, he's a crafty old fellow." They grinned amiably. "Fancy a swim?"

"I didn't bring my bathers."

"That has never bothered you before. Nothing like a bit of night skinny dipping." He saw her face and changed his tune. "Anyway, I'm sure you've left some bathers in the change rooms anyway."

"That was years and years ago Joel, and you know it. Metaphorically speaking, there has been a lot of water under the bridge since our early days of fun and innocence." She paused. "And skinny dipping for that matter."

"You were never fully innocent, my lovely one."

There was no adequate reply, and both knew it. Marcia went into the changing room to look for a demure, navy-blue one piece that she had always kept in case the old aunties came over. Surprisingly, it was still there, hanging on a brass hook. Her dear old dad hung onto the past, clinging onto those memories he treasured. She wanted rid of the past, and Joel wanted to start anew. It was confusing. The past, present, and future, didn't slide comfortably into any coherent whole.

Joel laughed warmly when he saw her in it, remembering the many frantic times when she had surreptitiously scrambled out of the pool to slide out of something more daring back into this old-maid one-piece bathing costume.

"When did you wear that last? I much prefer you in your skimpy black number," and with that, Joel pushed her playfully into the pool, unbuttoned his green shirt slowly, unzipped the fly of his cargo trousers, flamboyantly flew them over the deckchair, and stood for a brief second watching Marcia at the far end of the pool, watching him. He stood in his Calvin Klein black-and-white tight boxers, lavishing the fact that she was still, just watching. Him. Every bulge was conspicuous, and he stood, wondering if he should flick his boxers off, or not. He kept them on, as he dived expertly into the pool, swam the length under water, and came up for air, roughly pulling the thick straps off Marcia's shoulders.

He tugged the thick material down to her waist and clasped her to him, pulling her onto his lap. Her breasts lay tight on his expansive chest, his chest hairs rubbing against her smoothness. She felt his hardness against the top of her clothed thighs, and she lay back in the water as his hands were vigorously fondling her breasts.

Joel gently squeezed her breasts, then brought his mouth down first to suck one nipple quite hard, so that she pulled back, slightly, in delight. He then took the other nipple into his mouth, so gently, she winced out aloud, crying for more as he licked hungrily. Meanwhile, her hands were frantically grasping his firm muscular thighs, then they kept moving closer to grasping what she wanted to hold.

Joel backed her up against the wall of the pool, with his hardness pressing into her lower stomach, still covered with a thick barrier of her old-fashioned swimming costume. He kissed her like the Doctor Lion he was, on the prowl, hungry, starved for her mouth. She responded fully, a Doctor Pussy-Cat on heat, taking his bottom lip between her teeth, letting him devour her mouth, darting her tongue in and out of his mouth, familiarising herself with his taste.

Could two bodies ever desire each other this much? She was beside herself with need, a sexual urgency she had forgotten existed, particularly one like this, an all-encompassing demand. Her hands tried to push her bathing costume lower, willing him to take her fully, there in the pool, but his hands grasped hers just under the waist, as he whispered, "not yet my lovely one, not quite yet."

"Please Joel, take me, please do," she whimpered, desperate to be one with him and to be carried to sexual heights. As she went to grasp him, he swam away.

She pulled her straps back in place, and swam frantically after him. Years and years of swimming in this pool and at the beach, had made them strong swimmers, and she was frantic to reach him. Every time she drew closer to her reach, he swam away. Why? Nearly in tears, she arched her back, feeling like an angry spitting cat, but looking like an elegant dolphin coming out of the water, the top of the costume flopping loosely, its elastic worn with age. She dived on top of him.

Joel grabbed her to him and kissed her again, urgently, vigorously, on the mouth, his hands never moving far away from her breasts. Then, just as her body was moving in rhythm with his, ready, he withdrew, as he kept pulling her shoulder straps back up, and took her face in his hands. "You're beautiful Marcy. You are everything I have ever dreamt of in a woman."

"I really want you, Joel," cried Marcia, a tear slipping down her cheek.

Joel kissed her cheek softly. "I know darling, but I want more than just your adorable body." At this moment, Marcia wasn't sure what she wanted other than his incredible body.

They stood in the shower quietly in each other's arms. Joel, unashamedly in wet boxers, Marcia, still in her antiquated bathing costume. Then without a word, Joel went outside to dry off and to change, while she changed inside. She didn't have a clue what was happening.

When she came back outside, she thought she saw her father's study curtain move, but thought it must be her imagination playing tricks, her father had never been one to pry. Perhaps he was so desperate to find out what had been going on, but it wasn't like him to do so. She assumed she was imaging things. She went inside to make coffee. The night insects had come out, and Joel came inside, locking the patio door behind him.

Marcia set the coffee and cake out, and gently ruffled Joel's curls. How she had wanted to do that for a long time! He shook his head, knowing that his curls were uncontrollable. Usually, he cut it quite stylishly short. It needed a cut.

"I loved you touching me, Joel," she said quietly.

"Feeling good?"

"About as good as I've felt for so long."

They chatted affably until late, mainly about work individuals and colleague's foibles, deliberately steering clear of controversial topics.

Marcia was slightly peeved that Joel simply kissed her goodbye briefly, making no effort to arrange to see her on the weekend. She consoled herself with the thought that she had the ball to look forward to. For the first time for years, Marcia went home and to bed hugging herself, reassured in the knowledge that she was deeply desired.

I I

Why did Joel tease her in the pool? He could have made love to her, the opportunity was there, she had made herself available and her desire had matched his. What else did he want from her? He said he wanted more than just her body. She would have taken his body. What else did he want?

On Saturday, on the invitation of Joel's mother, Marcia called in to see his parents, Myra and Sam. Their house was modest, the same house that Joel had grown up in, but their hospitality was abundantly warm, as it always had been. The visit was important to ease her way back into meeting the rest of the family, and all the new additions to Joel's extended family. Myra and Sam were overjoyed to see her, they asked her no embarrassing or awkward questions, they simply showed her countless photos so that she could see how everyone had changed. Curiously, Marcia was relieved that Joel was not there. She was sure that was planned.

She didn't want people rushing to false conclusions about their relationship. What conclusion was there anyway? They weren't a couple? Not yet. Did going to the ball together change it? Perhaps. It was very public, quite out there for speculation. Perhaps not. She was merely accompanying him to a hospital occasion.

As she went to leave, Myra clutched her hand, and said, "your mother would be very proud of you, darling," and Marcia knew that no one other than Bill had known her mother as thoroughly as Joel's mother had done. How she missed her mother. She wanted to nestle into her maternal warmth like a girl again. With this compliment, she felt incredibly close to Myra, she always had, simply because of this lovely woman's loyal attachment to her mother, and that she had been present at every significant moment in her life, since a very young age.

After she left, she bought the last of her Christmas shopping, and feeling confident, she acted on a strange whim. She was still an old-school girl. She hadn't quite got used to this new Global Positioning System on the car. She accepted that in this day and age, it was ridiculous not to use a GPS, and it must be easy to try, but she was embarrassed to admit her ignorance and ask anyone for help. She wasn't techno-savvy. She could only use minimal functions on her smartphone. She didn't even know that her phone had an in-built GPS. Had she asked her father, even he could have helped her. He was proud of his new technological knowledge. He'd gone to a course with other senior citizens.

Instead, she took out her mother's old street directory out of her car glovebox, studied it carefully, and very deliberately, she drove to the street that still caused her so much heartache. As slowly as she could do without disturbing the flow of traffic, she drove down the street. At the end of the road, she parked, got out, looked up, contemplated walking it, and thought otherwise. What she had done today was an important first step in the right direction, and one she had needed to do alone.

She had a quiet night, and on Sunday, asked Joel to come over urgently. Dressing deliberately provocatively in a lovely, light, sheer summer frock, she waited impatiently until he came. He too was dressed in light cream colours, cream linen trousers, and a cream short sleeve shirt. His dark hair and tanned skin stood out markedly against the lightness of his clothes.

He didn't act as if he had hungrily embraced her in the pool two days ago. Rather, he was slightly distanced, and made no attempt to embrace her, noticing that Marcia's well-toned flesh was fully on display, her neckline exposing her bosom was almost too low, the back of her dress plunging deep down.

In a matter-of-fact tone, he asked, "well, what's this all about?"

Inwardly, Marcia was raging. She had hoped that he'd take one look at her in a sheer frock and want to cast it off. She wore the barest underwear underneath and suspected that Joel intuited this. Yet he made no move toward her. Why not? His mixed messages were confusing. Vixen-like, she wanted to lure him into her den, but she had called him over for a very specific task, and she adopted his standoffish manner, and went into cool overdrive. Her default position. Ice Maiden in person.

"Joel, would you do me a favour?"

"Of course."

"You trust me that clearly?"

"Eager to give me a reason not to?" There was no smile.

Ignoring this, she continued. "I want you to drive me to the street, you know the one, and walk up one side and down the other side."

"Fine, let's go. It's about time we did this."

"Wait, I've some more requests."

"Yes? What else?" He sounded impatient.

"Look, am I holding you up? Do you have another arrangement that I'm spoiling? Are you supposed to be elsewhere, with someone else?"

Now he was impatient. "No, just get on with it. You are making such a big issue of something that should be much more straightforward. Let's just go without the hysterics." He paused warily. "What other requests do you have?"

"I don't want you to speak to me, or touch me at all, or stop outside the restaurant."

"Grow up Marcia. I'm not accepting your terms."

"Please Joel, please, it's important to me."

"No, it's ridiculous, in fact, it's a bloody stupid suggestion. It's totally unnatural for me to walk down a tree-lined street with a beautiful woman, and not speak to her or touch her, particularly when she has deliberately worn a see-through dress that screams, 'touch me'."

Ignoring the obtuse compliment, she begged him, "please Joel, it's part of the process I need to go through."

"Shit Marcia, you should have gone through these processes years ago. You're a bloody doctor, you should know better than others that to suppress your emotions as much as you have, can only bring unnecessary stress. Straight after the tragedy, I had counsel with a brilliant psychologist. He was a great help to me. You should have done likewise."

"I thought I had dealt with the worst stuff, but it's one thing to do it in my mind, thousands of kilometers away from the place. Please Joel...," and she did what most women might do in that situation, she moved closer to him so that he could smell her perfume, put a hand on his thigh, pouted her lips coyly, in a way that was most unusual for her, and whispered, "please, Doctor Joel."

Seemingly unaffected, Joel replied, "I'll take you there gladly, walk you, hold your hand, talk to you, and buy you dinner."

"That's not what I want."

"Then it's not what I want. Seeya later, I'm off. I'll wait, just a bit longer for you to come to your senses," and Joel swivelled away without a word.

Marcia went racing past him and threw her arms around him. "Please Joel, do it for me."

"Marcia," he said robustly, clear resentment obvious in his voice. "I've done a lot of things for you over my life. Keeping away from you as requested was one of the more bizarre ones. Now, you throw your lovely body my way, then you make childish, juvenile requests to march ghostlike down the street that you should have walked down years ago. Grow up Marcia. Enter the real world, and that's not only being a good doctor. It's being a good person too, one that relates with warmth to those who care for you. Okay? When you understand what's involved in that, call me. See you tomorrow at work." With that, he was gone.

She sat quietly reflecting on his words. Admittedly, there were glimmers of wisdom there. She realised it, now. There were too many scary ghosts in her life that should have been exorcised long ago. Her father had begged her to see a psychologist, he'd recommended every good one he admired. She'd ignored his advice. She had tried to cope with trauma by disregarding the root of the pain, but it hovered, rarely far from the surface, returning to haunt her mind.

A new determination filled her. She quickly changed her clothes into a less provocative dress. She climbed into her sleek red car, drove to the significant tree lined street, parked where Joel had parked on the day he'd brought her here, got out, and found it easier to walk down it than she'd ever dreamt it might have been possible. If only she had established that earlier, she might have done it years back, and begun the healing journey.

"Doctor, heal thyself," she said aloud.

With each new shop or café or restaurant, she paused to look into the window, admiring the avant-garde clothes that she, with her classically elegant tastes, would never dare to wear. She poured over the innovative menus in the windows and inspected the out-lines of tasty gourmet food. She deliberately walked down the side of the street opposite to the side that had the one restaurant that still sent shivers down her spine. Crossing over, she looked down the street to gain its positioning.

With her bearing in mind, she walked a little faster, pausing to look in every window bar one – the one. The one capable of reducing her to a blubbering mess. The one at the root of her trauma. The one still causing a blockage in the relationship, between her and Joel. Two cafés down, she was astonished to hear familiar voices call her name.

"Hey Marcia, come and join us."

A group sat outside a café sipping different types of coffee and eating shared plates of delicate morsels. Una was there with some of the nurses she recognised but didn't know their names. Some clearly had partners with them, their arms around shoulders, looking cosy. To her amazement, Joel was part of the group. He clearly had left her house and come straight here anyway. She wondered whether he knew this group was here, or whether for his own purposes, he'd come back to the notorious street, and simply had bumped into them like she had. She hadn't seen his car in the street.

Una invited Marcia to join them, and looking at Una, she gasped. Oh, my word! In a shocking instant, she grasped for the first time what had nagged her sub-conscious about Una with her gorgeous long red curls and her lovely easy laugh. Oh my God! What a thing to recognise! Now, in this street. In this street of all places.

She looked so like Trish, the woman whose memory was attached to part of this street, part of what she was mentally blocking. How could it have taken her so long to see this? Her mind must be really screwed up.

"Marcia, are you alright?" Una asked kindly, picking up on the distress that was suddenly evident on Marcia's face.

"Yes, I'm fine, thank you," she answered more gruffly than she intended.

"Please join us," she asked again.

"No, thanks all the same, I've other plans for the afternoon." She caught Joel's look of disgusted disappointment at the quick lie she had told.

She didn't pause a moment longer to linger with the group of young professionals, sitting around on a lovely Sunday afternoon, relaxing, laughing, and enjoying life, but she went straight to her car and revved off home, surprising herself with her fast, unusually careless driving.

Reflecting on Joel's earlier impatience with her, all Marcia could think about was whether he'd had a prior arrangement to meet Una. If he did have this arrangement, why was he kissing her so passionately two nights back, ardently claiming her as his own, or at least, as the woman he desired at that moment in time? Did he desire another woman too? Was this why he didn't make love with her in the pool, even though her body had sent signals to let him know exactly what she wanted? If so, she couldn't cope with this. However, if she was even thinking like this, surely this was an admittance of more than a mere flimsy desire! Her desire was for real.

A certain relief flooded through her with this confession, as Marcia admitted her passionate craving for Joel. This was healthy. She'd studied psychology as part of their required undergraduate studies. The Professors had emphasised that denial can be such a repressive emotion, and there had been an abundance of this in her recent life. At the same time as this honesty rushed through her, disbelief overwhelmed her.

Marcia melodramatically hit her head with the open palm of her hand. Out aloud to her new sophisticated, minimalist furniture, she shouted, "I don't believe it. Yes, I do believe it." Her eyes rolled upward, outward, and ahead, not seeing anything but what was firmly fixed in her mind.

"I don't believe how stupid I've been. Una, the ravishing, red haired, close companion of Dr Joel Trucker, is the spitting image of the fiery, red headed, deceased Mrs Trish Trucker. That's why he's fallen for her. He accuses me of not dealing with the past, but he obviously needed someone whose resemblance is so striking to his first wife, I can't believe I've only just seen it." Marcia kept hitting her head.

She jumped up and grabbed her mobile phone and screamed into Joel's phone. "Who is Una, Joel? What has she got to do with Trish? Why did you never tell me the truth? Why did you have to wait and let me find out myself? Joel, tell me who is Una, and who am I to you?"

Marcia had no idea how many calls she made all through the afternoon. Joel didn't return her calls. She kept frantically checking her phone, hoping for a text or a call. Nothing came.

Surgery this week was going to be strained. Would she get any answers?

12

Marcia was caught in a quandary. The only way she was going to cope with the revelation about Una's likeness to Trish was to avoid Joel big time. But, she wanted, no, needed, to know the identity of Una. Who was she? Was she connected to Trish, that name she could hardly utter out aloud? Talk about a living contradiction. Avoidance and communication weren't happy bed-mates.

The morning surgery was a peculiar time. Everyone else was in wonderful moods; the ball was approaching. Christmas was around the corner, and the schedule for non-essential surgery had slowed down. Mid-January, the list for elective surgery was long.

Doctor Trucker's team were laughing and joking in-between the heavy concentration that was needed to operate, to assess a patient's progress, and to anaesthetise. As usual, Una and Joel were very relaxed with each other, their eyes flashing humour at every turn.

A junior nurse had even dared to put on a Christmas CD in the operating theatre, and she was dancing to and fro as she took the used instruments across to the steriliser. Typically, Joel only permitted classical music in his surgical theatre, but today, he allowed this jolly music as a Christmas concession. Una kept her eagle eye on this nurse who maintained her professionalism, despite the skip in her feet. Not once, did Una have to reprimand her for sloppy practices. She kept a tight, competent team.

The hospital was wonderfully decorated with Christmas trees, decorations, and the children's handmade ornaments. Everyone was as gay as can be in a hospital setting.

Marcia tried to avoid Joel. This was not easy. Then, when she could bear it no longer, no matter how hard she tried to communicate with Joel, he didn't respond. He was playing her frosty game. She was not used to that.

A breakthrough was necessary. First, she tried to appeal to him with her big blue eyes, but he just smiled back, not giving away any form of affection, and certainly not signalling any intimate desire. Every time she tried to grab him by the shirt, or by his jacket or ward coat, he broke away on the pretence of having to do something else in a rush.

"I'm busy Doctor," became his standard response as he strode manfully away.

"Too busy to talk with me?" she implored. He smiled innocently, and sauntered off, annoyingly handsome. In tune with his own rhythms. In control. Ever the King Lion, emperor of the hospital wards.

Despite the slower surgery schedule all through the hospital, where no child wanted to be during the festive season, unless they had to be, someone else was in the change rooms when they shared it at the end of their surgery schedules. Safety in numbers!

Furthermore, Joel no longer accompanied Marcia at the end of the day to the exit door, nor did he wait for her to leave as he did in the early days. Also, he was absent from her father's house in the evenings she visited. He left his answering machine on in the evening, choosing whose calls he returned. Hers was not one of them.

He had told her that he was casual with his use of mobile, using it only when essential. He rarely texted, messaged, or even called anyone, unless he absolutely had to. He kept his mobile for emergencies only. He was a face-to-face man, no techno freak. Marcia imagined that it was as though he had deliberately contrived to block her out of anything, but the briefest of essential, professional conduct.

Once, she confronted him on this. "Joel, are you avoiding me?"

"It's not fun, is it?" was his annoying response. This was strange. He wasn't a tit-for-tat sort of man.

Marcia was sorely tempted to visit him. She then hit her head with her hand. With some dismay and lots of personal embarrassment, she had to admit that she had not even had the courtesy to ask where he lived now. In her youth, not knowing where he lived would have been unthinkable, she would have visited him countless times, but she was no longer a mere wisp of a girl. There had been too much of a life gap for her to jump across the ditch without slipping into the muddy waters, not knowing how to scramble out.

She was also desperate to know Una's real identity, and why Joel was intimate with someone so physically, and in temperament, like his deceased wife. An emotional tiredness pressed in on her, and she knew she had to preserve energy for the pantomimes on Thursday, Friday, and Saturday nights, followed on Saturday, by the much talked about hospital ball.

Marcia's emotions were in a whirl. Why wasn't Joel taking Una to the ball? Why had he asked her? Working with Joel was proving to be more difficult than she had ever imagined, and from day one, she had known that it would be emotionally hard.

He was even more attractive with age and maturity than she ever remembered in his self-assured, somewhat brash youthfulness. Now, his face conveyed the self-confident authority that in his youth she interpreted as merely impertinent cockiness, but Marcia had watched many women misinterpret his pleasant easiness, as flirtatiousness.

Women didn't realise that he was friendly and warm to all women, regardless of their looks or marital status. He was a man who genuinely loved women. That he also had an enviable comfortable manner with men also, was an asset in a doctor. She had to give it to him, he never put the male nurses down, but he encouraged them, just as he did the female nurses. This man was amazing, she mused.

But he was avoiding her. She felt this loss of contact like a deep gut pain.

She had to do something for light relief. To her massive surprise, Jo-Belle phoned her. "Hi darling, it's Jo-Belle here, long time, no see."

"Hiya Jo-Belle, where on earth did you get my number from?"

"Nice greeting, I've missed you too. My latest partner has a kid who goes to the school you're doing the pantomime in, and she thought your name rung a bell, so she asked that boring teacher for your number. So, darling, what have you been up to?"

"What have you been up to?"

"Oh, I've probably had about a hundred women since we saw each other last, but I think I've got one who's a keeper at long, bloody last."

"You're lucky."

"Yeah, I am. Now sweetheart, I know all about the wretched accident, and how you took off up north, leaving your buddies behind, so tell me a bit about what you're doing back here. How's that gorgeous doctor you always fancied? If I wasn't a lesbian, I'd have the hots for him." This made Marcia giggle.

Jo-Belle was a patient listener, and Marcia found her extremely easy to talk with. She asked the right sort of questions about her time in the north of Australia, without stepping on her toes. She found herself opening up, spilling the beans, like she had never done with anyone. It was liberating to admit to someone how much she desired Joel, and Jo-Belle gave her sound advice on how to communicate her attraction. They talked for ages and Marcia felt every bone in her body relax.

Jo-Belle signed off, "go get him love, that hunk has always wanted you, and he was the one you should have grabbed the first-time round. You listen to me."

These words of advice left Marcia musing deeply. She wished she hadn't prejudged this friend. She was great fun to chat with and very helpful too. Quickly, she saved her number while she remembered how to do it. Why was she clever at everything medical, and so hopeless at technical know-how?

Now, back at hospital, Marcia watched Joel as he once had watched her, daily, hourly, every minute of the day she could, watched him being friendly to all and sundry, and to no one in particular, except for the sexy, sultry Una who arrived in his car many mornings, and often left with him in the afternoons. The pattern wasn't the same each week. She couldn't work it out.

It was a most peculiar lead up to the Christmas ball. As staff sat around during morning coffee and lunch, nurses and doctors together, Marcia half listened to the women chatter excitedly about their new frocks. She kept quiet about the dress she'd bought. Jo-Belle had persuaded her, or she'd never have bought it had she been by herself. They had a great day out together. It was the first time she'd had a girly day out since her mother had died. They had laughed her tensions away.

Desperately trying to catch Joel's eyes, all he did was smile at her, in the same way as he did when he caught anyone looking at him. He was infuriatingly kind to everyone. Wasn't she special? Was she?

Marcia felt hypocritical. She was avoiding Joel. But that wasn't what she wanted. Marcia started to believe that his escaping of her was a form of tortuous seduction, that in not having any physical contact, or even personal, verbal dialogue, other than strictly, essential medical discussions, by the end of the week, she would be beside herself with longing, and simply hurl herself at him.

If this was his intention, it was working. He was acting as the Lion, the King of the Jungle, the royal hospital sovereign. She'd crawl into his den any day.

In desperation, Marcia even started hunting for detailed medical cases and questions to explore with him, anything for an excuse to bend her head close to his, to have the occasional brush of his hand against hers as he turned the case notes back, but there were insufficient complex cases to deal with during these lean surgical times. When she did raise a medical concern with him, he dismissed all her queries in a typical masculine off-handedness that was an affront to her expertise, as well as to her fragile ego.

On Thursday, she was due to do her first performance of Cinderella. The question of Una's identity and her resemblance to Trish nagged her constantly. At last, at the end of the day, she waited for Joel as inconspicuously as she could, near the exit.

As soon as she saw him approach, she jumped out. "Joel, I'd like to talk."

"Ha ha, you're a nice one to suggest that," and he laughed flippantly and went to walk away.

Marcia clasped his shirtsleeve firmly, feeling his taut muscles beneath her clammy fingers, the touch raising her pulse. "Please Joel, why are you avoiding me?"

Joel harshly shrugged her hand away, and again laughed, this time, with a mocking sound. "It's fine for you to avoid me, and ignore my interest in you, but not so fine the other way around, hah?" His eyebrows shot up as he asked the pointed question and stood facing her as obstinately as she faced him. His dark eyes melted when he saw the warmth of her blue eyes. "Look darling, the beautiful Cinderella tonight, I'll see you tomorrow at the hospital, then soon, you will be my Cinderella. I certainly will not be avoiding you forever."

"So, you admit you're avoiding me?"

"Not really Marcia. This is a pathetic waste of our time."

Marcia stepped closer to him. They were just a hand span away. She inhaled his familiar musk smell and painfully sighed, "Joel, please tell me about Una."

At that precise moment, a woman jumped out of the shadows, grabbed Joel from behind, and nestled into his side. "What's this about Una? Who's plotting about me?" And she chuckled with Joel.

As usual, Joel took full control. "What makes you think I would bother to plot about you, you fine filly? Enjoy tonight, Marcia, I'm sure you'll make a fabulous Cinderella, and I'll see you at work to-morrow," and with that, he was gone, one arm loosely around Una's trim waist.

Infuriated and fuming, Marcia stormed off in the direction of her car and headed off to school. That Joel was so totally in com-mand of his emotions and his relationships annoyed her because she knew how thoroughly a victim of her mixed passions she felt.

The last person in the world she wanted to see tonight was Clive Burns. However, Clive greeted her enthusiastically, and Marcia felt a slight twinge of meanness at how rude she responded in return. She just couldn't be bothered explaining what she was going through in any way, let alone in the details that Clive would have tried to claw out of her. He adored petty gossip.

The pantomime was a great success, as Marcia knew it would be. The school hall was not quite full, although she knew that Friday was a sell-out. Marcia went through the motions of the play, smiling at Clive, but keeping a firm grip on his shoulders as he danced the finale with her. Afterwards, she was cool, distant, and made her exit hurriedly, but not so quickly that she could not see his down-cast face.

The next workday followed a similar pattern. At the hospital, Marcia tried earnestly to connect with Joel in ways that went beyond the barest, minimal discussion over essential medical details, but now he was playing Marcia's avoidance game to the full. Was it her game? Had he learnt the rules from her? Surely not.

Not that she was ever distracted from her immediate tasks of helping sick children, but in every spare minute of the day, walking from theatre to the wards, or down hospital corridors to the coffee room, one subject preoccupied her, a man of infinite charm, of astonishing looks, of indisputable charisma, and with a body she lusted after.

He had always been a natural part of her life, except for those horrible years. She wanted him back, so she thought. Would she ever get him?

13

Joel had not even bothered to finalise the arrangements for collecting Marcia from the school pantomime. This made her feel jittery, as if he might pull out of taking her. When she broached it with him, he was off hand.

"I'll pick you up, it will work out fine."

"When Joel? What time?"

"When I'm ready." He was trying to be casual, indifferent even, it was frustrating her. She couldn't understand it. This was not the old Joel.

Marcia was seriously flustered with the idea of rushing from pantomime mode for children, straight to ball mode with adults. It was a massive head spin. Could she do it?

No matter how many times she tried to rehearse in her mind how to plan the evening carefully in terms of removing thick, theatrical make up, showering, and applying glamorous evening make up, it always seemed to be a messy picture.

She had tried her new dress on several times, experimented with her hair, practised new make-up techniques, but she still felt amateurish in the art of sophisticated glamour. Such dressing up reminded her too closely of her youth. She missed her mother's helpful suggestions. Her mother had always looked wonderful, fresh, elegant, fashionable, in a quiet self-confident manner.

The realisation that Joel hadn't even seen her made up for a glamorous night out for all these years, scared her. The thought of the night when he'd last seen her fully made up frightened her even more.

Only once, over morning tea, a junior nurse asked, "what are you wearing to the ball, Dr Knight?"

"Ah, you'll have to wait and see," she teased. Joel was at the end of the table, appearing not to hear or to notice her. He was doing a superb job of avoiding her. Marcia couldn't work it out. He appeared not to even raise his eyes from the newspaper he was reading. She wondered what he was thinking. Would he be recalling the last night she'd dressed up for him?

The nurse persisted. "What about a hint? What colour is it?"

"A colour I don't wear often." At this, Joel raised his eyes for a second before dropping them again. Marica wondered why. She could not work him out. There was a time when she had understood every glance of the eyes, every raise of the eyebrows, every hand gesture or facial glance. Had so much changed?

The Friday night performance brought a surprise. Myra and Sam came with a large group of their grandchildren. Marcia didn't recall telling Myra about the play, so she assumed that Joel had bought the tickets for his nieces and nephews. He loved kids. He'd be a great uncle. She peered into the darkness of the hall, looking in vain for him, but while she saw a sea of faces, she failed to see the one face that haunted her dreams. Nightly, he flew in and stayed. On those nights, she slept well, seeing his face, feeling his arms comfort her, his lips close to hers.

After the night's successful pantomime performance, she kept her Cinderella gown on and made a quick visit to the audience to greet Joel's parents and grandchildren. As well as Joel's nieces and nephews, there were two of his sisters-in-law who she vaguely recalled meeting. Everyone was chattering with great delight. They had loved the play, especially the wonderful Cinderella. They touched her gown as if it was the finest silk, satin, and lace.

Then she made a hasty exit. The second she walked into her apartment, her phone rang. "Hello Cinderella, my darling."

"Hello Joel." She hoped her voice sounded sufficiently cool, suppressing the rush of excitement that flowed through her very being the second she heard his voice, and the magic words "my darling."

"I hear you make a pretty gorgeous Cinderella." They laughed easily, she knew that his mother would have phoned him as soon as she could, reporting all the relevant details. Myra was a great one for the chat. "Are you all ready for tomorrow?"

"I really wish I didn't have to do a performance before."

"No, my darling, let me tell you, the real performance comes after."

"What an earth do you mean?" A rush of nervousness filled her.

He ignored her question. "I'll pick you up after the panto, rush you back home to change, and we'll take it from there."

"Do you always ignore my questions?"

Quick as a flash, Joel asked, "do you always ignore my desires?" and he gave her no chance to rebut him. "See you tomorrow." He hung up. He was playing an aloof game. This was not like him at all. It made her nervous.

Marcia had to be content with the promise of the next night, and methodically proceeded to lay everything she needed in the spare bedroom. She painted her nails blood red and put a glossy sealer over them. It was the first time she had painted her nails since that night, the one she was forever trying to forget. Her fingers looked strange, different, as if they weren't an extension of her hand, but they belonged on someone's else's hands.

She was relieved that she didn't need to work at the hospital this Saturday. If she did, anything other than the essential anaesthesia techniques would be a blur. She floated through Saturday as in a trance.

She called Joel. He answered immediately. "Is everything alright?"

"Yes, I'm nervous."

"What about?" He sounded gruff.

"Tonight."

"What about tonight?"

"Moving my headspace from a pantomime with children, to a ball with you."

"So, what's bothering you? The ball or going with me?" She was relieved with his blunt question. It helped her.

"Both."

"Why, Marcy?"

It all burst out. "I'm going to be in one outfit for the children, then rushing back to change. I haven't been out to a ball since university days. I've hardly been anywhere glamorous for so long." She paused as if she wanted to say more.

"Is that it?"

"No, there is more."

Joel let a long silence hover before asking, "what else is bothering you?"

"Don't get frustrated with me."

"What's bothering you?"

"What are people going to think seeing us together?"

Joel laughed. "So, that's what's truly worrying you, isn't it?"

"No, it's not really unsettling me, I just don't know how people will respond."

"Stop worrying, it'll be fine. I must go, Cinderella, I'll seeya tomorrow. Don't lose your slipper." He didn't even wait for a shared chuckle but hung up.

Nervous anticipation raced through Marcia as she dressed for the last finale of the pantomime performance. As she stepped onto the stage in her scruffy brown dress with some ragged edges and one shoulder exposed, the lights panned quickly over the audience, and she gasped out aloud. Never in her daydreams had she stopped to think that Joel might bother to come and watch her act in a school play. In their medical school days, they had both been on the stage together, but that was a long time ago. Way back in the distant past. They had even played Romeo and Juliet on stage, as well as in real life.

Had he purchased a ticket? Maybe he'd charmed his way in, or realistically, he'd probably bought a final performance ticket when he'd bought the tickets for his relatives. If he had bought a ticket, way was he standing? Now, he stood leaning tantalisingly on the back wall in his evening-wear, looking as if he owned the place, or at least everything desirable in it.

Trying to block the vision of this handsome man was not an easy task, nor was dancing in the arms of Clive Burns, when the man she would later dance with was in full view. The final applause was loud, the children's excitement uncontainable, as they went off chatting and giggling to their end of concert party.

Marcia applied cold cream liberally to her face, scrubbing off the garish stage paint. With relief, she threw off the wedding dress that had so thrilled the children, and she donated it to the school's collection of costumes. She quickly pulled on lightweight trousers and a tee-shirt. Outside the dressing room, a clamour of noise greeted her, but nothing distracted her now.

Joel properly extracted himself from the tedious celebrations of Clive, who was delighted with the three encores they had received, and Joel put a guiding arm around Marcia's waist, to steer her through the throngs toward his car.

"Joel," Marcia began tentatively, looking down at her casual clothes and looking up at his smoothly shaven face, then slowly looking him up and down, in an admiring fashion that was more typical of a man. "You look absolutely fantastic." She put one hand on his shoulder, feeling the tactile texture of the quality, black jacket, playfully twitched his black bow tie, ran a hand coquettishly over his starched white cotton shirt, then quickly slid a hand down his inner thigh.

Joel grabbed this hand and hastily thrusted aside. "Come my Cinderella, come to the real ball, but first we need your transformation."

They drove in silence, not an altogether uncomfortable silence, more a nervous air of anticipation, like a dense fog around them was holding them in, but not letting them surface for air. The sun was yet to break through the clouds. It was trying, some bright rays were piercing through.

As they drove into her apartment block, Joel reached over and patted her hand. "You were a brilliant Cinderella for the kids, now don't be nervous Marcia. Let's enjoy tonight fully."

"Who's nervous?" she responded more irritably than she wanted to sound. Marcia's nerves were shot to pieces. She had not dressed up and been out with a man since that fateful night five years ago. She'd forgotten normal dating customs. But that's absurd she thought. Is this what is happening? Am I dating Joel? He's an old mate, a family friend, that's all. How wrong she knew this was. He was her heartthrob, the man she desired with a bursting passion.

Joel took it for granted that he would come in with her, and then, sensitive man he was, he guessed her unease. "Now, where would you like me to go?"

"You stay here Joel," and she steered him into the lounge. "And Joel?"

"Yes?" His eyes danced in glee.

"No peeping until I'm ready." With that request, the dashing

Prince Charming gave a playful bow of acquiescence, and Marcia scuffled off to set in motion what she had practised in the right order.

In haste, she showered, pulled on a silk dressing gown, applied make-up more glamorously than she had applied it for years, and twisted her hair into a chignon. It was now sufficiently long enough to sit in place, and she pushed a long diamante pin through the lengths to hold the roll in place, pulling a few curly tendrils loose to soften the image. She placed small, red ruby earrings on her lobes, thinking wistfully of her mother. The earrings had been her mother's, a wedding anniversary gift from her beloved spouse, Marcia's father. With the numerous experiments of trial dressing up during the week, she had decided against wearing a necklace, preferring to leave her neck fully exposed to the wonder of her dress.

The purchase of this dress was the most audacious item of clothing she had ever worn. She and Jo-Belle had had a ball shopping for it. They'd made it a day out and lunched afterward. Typically, Marcia was quite conservative in taste, preferring understated, stylish, timeless garments. Jo-Belle was outrageously outlandish, hence the choice of this dress.

Even now, as she stepped into the frock, she was astonished at her daring. It transformed her appearance from a classically beautiful, but rather plainly dressed professional, to a sexy, saucy siren, a James Bond seductress. She hoped that by wearing the dress, her personality also would suitably adjust, and she would be transformed from a cool, detached, quiet woman, an Ice Maiden, to a fiery, engaged, arousing, cat-woman. That's what her lesbian friend said would happen. She seemed to know these things.

Her painted red nails sparkled as she smoothed the red satin dress over her slim hips. She took a last look at her cleavage. There was no time to wonder whether her breasts were too fully exposed. They were. She looked away. The dress was slinky and tight with thin straps, a deep vee-neckline and back, and tight over the waist and hip. The hemline was full-length, and up the right side, a long split ran the full stretch of her thigh, a sparkling diamante clasp drew attention to her exposed, shapely leg. She slipped into high, white, strappy sandals, put her trademark red lipstick on, sprayed an overgenerous amount of Chanel Five over her skin, and took a deep breath. She walked into the lounge, feeling hyper-sexy.

She caught Joel off-guard. He was reading a medical magazine of hers. He looked up as he heard her door open, and simply sat spellbound for seconds, totally speechless. His eyes roamed wildly and unashamedly over her voluptuous body.

"Well?" asked Marcia, bemused at his response, but needing some affirmation of his approval.

"My God, Marcia," and he hesitated, looking for the right words, his eyes hardly believing what they were seeing. Then, in a tone she wasn't ready for, he asked, "what are you trying to do?"

"What do you mean?" Her face clouded; this was not the response she had expected.

Joel stood up, walked over to her, breathed in her perfume, and almost seemed lightheaded with its fragrance. "Marcia, you look abundantly sexy."

"Is that okay?" she asked coquettishly.

Joel smiled vaguely. She couldn't interpret it. His answer was slow and deliberate. "Yes and no. Yes, on my behalf, I love that you look so desirable, and no, it's not okay on behalf of all the other men whose eyes will be glued to places on your body I wish they weren't."

"It's not too provocative, is it?" asked Marcia confused, looking down at herself, and now, seeing ample flesh, neck, shoulders, arms, breasts, and legs. She hadn't felt so totally feminine and desirable for such a long time. Seduction was powerful. Suddenly, she was in command, and Joel was in her hands, a body to be moulded to her desires. Yes, she would enjoy the night to the full. She would play the role of sexy seductress, cat-woman, no Ice Maiden.

Her body leaned up against his and she felt its masculine strength. Surprisingly, Joel moved away. In almost a sad voice, he asked, "what made you want to dress this outrageously, Marcia?"

This was not what she had expected. She had assumed that Joel would love to see her dressed like a sex siren, but she refused to be put off. Not tonight. It had taken a massive burst of new courage to be persuaded by her girlfriend to purchase this dress. The dress was a deliberate ploy on her part. He couldn't avoid her whilst she was dressed like this. The dress screamed, "touch me, everywhere."

Instead of emphasising this, she answered thoughtfully. "Daddy never let me dress in anything other than classic simplicity, much like mummy, and Rob seemed to prefer that conservative style too."

"Marcia, that's the first time you've mentioned Rob."

With a dismissive shrug, Marcia simply said, "well there, I've said it now," and she proceeded to gyrate into his pelvis, but he backed off, unsure of how to respond to her showing off with this new image. It wasn't that he could resist being highly turned on, for he was. Indeed, part of his moving away was that she wouldn't detect how aroused he had become, but it was early in the night, and, if there was to be a seduction, Joel wanted the lead up to be slow and lingering, not just an act of explicit physical lust. He was quite the romantic at heart. He always had been and hoped he always would be.

A car horn sounded, and Joel pulled Marcia outside, explaining that he had ordered a taxi because they would be drinking champagne and he couldn't drive home.

14

The ball was in full flight when they arrived. Couples dressed in their summer finery were floating around the hall, in the arms of someone they liked or loved or lusted after, or for a few, weren't sure how they felt. The second Joel and Marcia stepped inside the hall, faces turned toward them, then away. Marcia noted with secret delight the way that men and women looked almost in shock at her dress. Certainly, there were other women wearing revealing gowns, and others who were beautiful in their own ways.

Tonight, Marcia was Belle of the Ball. She had the height to carry off such a sleek, elegant, slinky dress. Her blonde chignon gave her further height. She suspected that whoever accompanied the stunningly handsome Dr Joel Trucker to the ball would stand out, simply by being on his arms. His tall frame, his powerful shoulders, his way of steering her authoritatively through the throngs, while throwing out a casual greeting to passers-by, made him a central character. Everyone seemed to know him. People moved aside to let them pass through, as if they were celebrities. Marcia felt special.

While Marcia was loving the unaccustomed attention, it was making her feel decidedly nervous. Of what, she wasn't entirely sure. To cope with her nerves, she drank a flute glass of champagne quickly, wanting the bubbles to go straight to her head, enjoying the feeling of sheer and utter light-hearted carefreeness after years of hard work, inner pain, and suppressed sentiment.

Joel's hand never left her side, or sometimes her lower back, as he steered her here and there to greet this group, and then that group. His hand was familiar, a comfort, slowly calming her nerves.

Then, they were on the dance floor. The band played some quick jazz and Joel swirled Marcia to and fro, in and out, back and forth. It was such fun. They had learnt dancing together as young teenagers, at classes after school, paid for by Marcia's mother. The dance moves came back to them readily, easily, as if they danced together every day. Their eyes sparkled.

"Do you remember dancing in my bedroom as kids?"

"Sure do. Do you remember dancing around the pool as teenagers?"

"Sure do." She didn't keep the reminiscing going, leaving their dancing together at university as students, unsaid.

The dancing was exhausting, they were putting on a performance, just as Joel had predicted. Eyes from the sidelines and the dance floor were on them. They stood out. Joel was an athletic man. Marcia was a bit tired through having done the three school performances at night, and she tired quicker than he did. But adrenaline kicked in, and they made an impressive couple on the dance floor.

"Enjoying it, Marcy?" he asked as he leant into her as the music was changing, and he placed a daring kiss deep in her cleavage. She shivered with joy as his lips met her skin. Not once, did she wonder who saw.

Tonight, she didn't react negatively to his endearment. "I'm having so much fun. I haven't danced for years. I just need to take a short break."

They sat down, and Marcia kept gulping down champagne too quickly. She still was a bundle of nerves. They sat close, but not as a couple, Joel's arm wasn't around her shoulder. Whereas, on the dancefloor, in his arms, she had felt she was his partner in a full sense.

Joel left her briefly, and immediately, she felt agitated. It was almost as if a panic attack struck her. She had taken his presence for granted, and men she hadn't seen at the hospital swooped in the second he was gone. She tried to be cool, laughing off their compliments on her sexiness, and most took the hint, and moved on. But one stayed, pawing her leg. She slapped his hand, but not too hard. He rose just as Joel returned. Instead of the sympathy she thought she would get from him, he was abrupt.

"Why wear that sort of dress Marcia if you don't want men to touch you?"

"Why should men think they have the right to touch me just because I'm wearing this sort of dress?"

"Because they do."

"That's pathetic."

"Maybe, but it's true."

She was cross. "I don't believe we're having this conversation in this day and age." Marcia stood up and looked at him in disbelief. "I really thought you'd like me in this dress."

Joel stood up, his height towering above her. He gently took her hands in his. "I adore you in this dress Marcia, but I'd adore you in a dress that didn't let the whole world see your gorgeous body."

"I thought you'd like to see my body."

"I do, but I want more than your body. When will you grasp this?"

"I need more champagne."

"You don't."

"I don't like you telling me what I do or don't need."

"You never did listen to me, Marcia," and with that, she was off somewhat unsteadily on her high heels, in pursuit of some more bubbly.

Marcia had drunk a lot. Usually, as a doctor, she was a moderate, occasional drinker. Often, she'd go for weeks without a sip of wine. She never drunk alone, and she'd been by herself for years. Now, in the crowd, she couldn't find her way back to Joel. Men kept touching her, trying to get her back onto the dance floor. Once, she yielded, and found herself in the arms of one of the senior cardiac consultants. He was an older man who was still very good-looking. Without the drink in her, she probably wouldn't have stayed in his arms for very long.

She was thrust from one man's arms to the next one who claimed her, always looking in vain over her shoulders for Joel. The music had slowed considerably, and the radiographer who now had taken possession of her, couldn't take his eyes off her breasts pushed up against his jacket.

At last, she caught sight of Joel far away in the distance, and she left the radiographer's arms and fought her way through the crowds, only to see him swaying on the dancefloor with Una. This was the first time that Marcia had seen Una tonight. How lovely she looked, also in red, but a deep orange red, complimenting her hair. Marcia sat back, trying to ease herself into a seat where no one could interrupt her. She watched thoughtfully as Joel and Una easily sunk into each other's bodies as if they were made for each other.

Una was uncannily like Trish. She could have been Trish. Watching them was like watching the husband-and-wife she once painfully knew, Joel and Trish, but now Joel and Una. What was going on? Why had Joel invited her to the ball, and not Una? Surely, they were married. Suddenly, tipsy, her mind was muddled, but feeling more sober than she was, she stood and made a rapid search for the exit.

The couple waltzed over to her as they saw Marcia trying to escape, but Joel grabbed her arm so tightly that she winced in pain.

"Where are you going?"

"Away, to let you dance with your Trish look-alike."

"I don't believe you, Marcia," Joel said in amazement. "Una and I debated vigorously whether to tell you or not about us, but we decided to let you find out for yourself. You haven't really bothered."

Marcia was fighting to restrain tears. "Find out what?"

At this moment, a pleasant looking man came across and gave Una an enormous bear hug, apologised for being late, and whisked her off to the dance floor. Una threw over her shoulders, a hasty, "Marcia, you look a winner. For goodness' sake Joel, tell her, I'm sick of the hide-and-seek nonsense."

Joel grabbed Marcia's shoulders roughly and spun her around so that she was facing him. His rugged, handsome face was raging red. "Listen here, Doctor Knight, formerly Doctor Collins, formerly Miss Marcia Newton."

"Why throw these names in my face now? Why tonight?"

"Because it's highly relevant. Right from the start, you've been so damn rude to Una, I can't believe it. All she's ever been to you is generous, warm, and sensitive."

"Joel, are you in love with her? Is that what you are trying to tell me?"

"God Marcia, I cannot believe you."

"I can't believe you."

"Do you see the man she is dancing with?" Hands around her waist, with noticeable aggression, Joel spun her around again, but this time so that she was facing the dance floor. He leaned into her back, feather kissing her neck, and whispered into her ear, "that man is her dearly beloved husband, to whom she is in very early stages of pregnancy." He let this sink in, kissed her lightly again, and spun her needlessly roughly back to face him. "She lives near to me which is why we often travel to work together."

Marcia's face was screwed in confusion. "What's your relationship to her? Why does she look so much like Trish?"

Joel was quiet, his tanned face had gone pale, as in fright. "Come outside."

It took time to meander through the throngs. People wanted to speak to them. Joel was single-minded, looking for a quiet spot. There were not many to be found. Many other couples had chosen to come outside for a breather. It was a warm night.

"Marcia, Una is..." and he paused, trying to find the right words. "Perhaps I should say, was Trish's twin. They weren't identical, they were fraternal twins, but they are very alike anyway."

"A twin? I never knew Trish was one."

"No, I get that. Una was back in Ireland for a long stretch visiting her grandparents and getting experience in Irish hospitals. I never got to know her when I was going out with Trish. Una was having medical treatment for a rare disease that Irish consultants are world leaders in. That's why she couldn't come to the wedding. She was in the middle of crucial treatment that couldn't be interrupted. I suggested we delay the date. Trish was heartbroken, but we agreed to go ahead with the wedding, and we had planned a trip to Ireland later to visit her. This never eventuated, for reasons you know." He paused, letting this sink in.

"How come I never heard Trish talk about a twin sister?"

"Why would you? Una was in Ireland for years. I hadn't met her myself."

"Oh, go on." Marcia couldn't wait to hear where the story was heading.

"Apart from your father and my mother, Una is the most important person in my life in helping me to come to grips with my loss. She too lost something precious, a sister, and a twin no less. When I first met her, I was astounded at the similarity of gestures, mannerisms, and likeness. We assumed that you would see that instantly." Joel was struggling with the story. He kept pausing to make sure Marcia was absorbing the details.

"Wow Joel, I had no idea."

"At the start, when she first sought me out in Melbourne to talk to me, I was shocked by the likeness. It was uncanny. Even if they're not identical, it freaked me out. That's why I can't believe you didn't see it and start to ask questions. Anyway, she came to me hoping that I could help her, as obviously, I was the last one to spend time with her sister, and she wanted to know more details about her. Initially, I found it excruciatingly hard, they look so alike that memories inevitably flooded back. I can't believe you've taken so long to see it."

"Now, I can't believe it myself." Marcia was subdued.

"Then, increasingly, I appreciated Una's help, often just in having the chance to reminisce with someone who is so understanding. She told me lots that I didn't know about Trish's childhood, and this helped me understand many of her quirks. Una and Neville are wonderfully in love." Marcia could see that, they had eyes only for each other, their bodies dancing appeared like peas in a pod, they were clearly made for each other. "You ask about my relationship with Una. My relationship with her is like having a close sister, I guess I still see her as my sister-in-law, and that's how I relate to her. That's why I can occasionally kiss and cuddle her, I do so as if she's one of my sisters. You know how affectionate I am with them. I'm extremely fond of Una. I've seen your horrible jealous looks every time I am near her."

Marcia was speechless. Joel's face bore signs of the deep pain he had carried for years, but had, with Una's help, worked through its negative consequences. Somehow, he had managed to bear the agonising grief of loss in a way that allowed him to move on, without every forgetting the lingering pain.

"How do you never betray your sadness in public, Joel? Is it an act?"

"How dare you suggest that, Marcia? You really can be thought-less." His face darkened.

"I'm sorry, I didn't mean it that way."

"Then what did you mean?" Frustration was evident in his voice. "This wasn't an easy story to account."

"I know. But you're so cheery to everyone, do you drop your bundle and be morose at home?"

"Lonely yes, sad most definitely, reflective of regrets, but not morose. Life has to flow on, and quickly I discovered that there is more pleasure in being pleasant to people, than in being grumpy."

"Are you casting aspersions my way?" Marcia scowled.

Joel shook his head. "Stop interpreting things negatively. Be positive Marcia. As your father keeps saying to you, grasp life in all its rich fullness, that's all I'm trying to say. I've had to work at it, of course I have, however it looks, none of this has come easy to me. Una has been marvellous in helping me to stay hopeful, despite the pain of loss we both have experienced."

"Take me home to bed, Joel."

"I'll take you home, but not to bed."

"Why not Joel? Don't you desire me? Don't you ever want to make love to me?" The effects of the drink had returned, now the shock of the discovery of Una's identity had been revealed.

He ignored her question. "Are you up to a last dance?"

"Of course," and Marcia made a weak effort to move back inside where the music was slow, romantic, and only the serious dancers were left.

Joel held Marcia tightly as they swayed slowly, hardly moving, and Marcia almost fell asleep on his shoulders.

"Come, my love, home to bed."

"Yes please," murmured Marcia in delight.

15

Light streamed through white linen curtains as Marcia opened her eyes. Looking about her, she saw a neat bedroom decorated in a traditional style of recycled pine furniture to match the polished wooden floorboards that appeared original. White, high-quality furnishings made an impressive mark. She assumed she must be in Joel's house. She hadn't remembered falling asleep. Strange, she never would have guessed that he would have chosen to live in an old, renovated, stone cottage. It almost had a rustic feel to it, not in any rough and ready sense, but in a sophisticated, classy way. Her choice was for the new, ultra-postmodern, minimalist, and shiny. Very Sydney.

Suddenly conscious of a figure in the doorway, she sat up, aware for the first time that she was only wearing her red, lace, strapless bra and panties. The good-looking man in the doorway stood leaning on the distressed pine door frame. My God, he was handsome. He wore a long white towelling bathrobe, untied. He ran his fingers slowly, unintentionally seductively, through his damp hair. Marcia was excited at the image.

"Where's my dress?"

"That's a fine greeting. It's hanging up."

"Did you take my dress off?"

Joel laughed. His smile came easily, it slid out without trying. "Believe me, you were in no form to take it off yourself." Marcia's sore head was testimony to this fact.

Joel sauntered casually over to the bed, and no matter how hard Marcia tried, she couldn't avoid gazing at the space where his robe hung open. Rising out of the bed, her desire mounted, and she reached out to grasp his body, clasping his waist. He pushed her back onto the bed, opened his robe fully, and lay flat on top of her. Their lips met with a fierce passion, both equally as hungry for each other. Marcia's hands were crazily trying to pull off her briefs, but Joel held her down.

"Joel, I want you," screamed Marcia, desperation vivid in her cry. He ignored her shout and continued to hold her down. "Joel, let me go, rip my underwear off, please, don't torture me any longer, take me, I'm all yours."

"You're not mine Marcy, you are still your own, and until I know you're mine, you cannot have me, it is as straight-forward as that," and so saying, he rolled away, and lay beside her, but not for long. Marcia leapt on top of him, feeling his desire firm beneath her. Joel's hands clasped her buttocks and panties tightly, refusing to allow her to remove them. The more arduously she kissed him, the firmer she felt him grow, so that she felt she would explode if he didn't make love with her immediately.

Instead, he threw her off, and, holding his robe over him, trying to cover what couldn't be disguised, he left the room. Marcia raced after him.

"What sort of man are you, Joel? I'm lying there, all yours, and you won't even take me. I can't believe it." Her hands were racing over his body, still enclosed in the bathrobe. She was frantic, a woman possessed, her body sweated with the heat of desire, and she unclasped her bra and threw it over her shoulder. Before she could pull her panties off, Joel again grasped her hands. He picked her up and threw her back onto the bed. Thinking this meant that he was about to make love to her, Marcia reached out to grasp him around the neck, but he slipped out of her hands.

Standing back from her, his robe now closed tightly and firmly tied at the waist, he quietly said, "have a shower, Marcy. I put clothes out for you. They were Trish's, I'm sorry, but I've no other suggestions for what you could wear, for the moment. I've kept a few of her things, not a lot, just a few random items. I know you used to borrow each other's clothes sometimes, so I hope they will do for now."

"Joel, why wouldn't you take me?" Marcia lay back in bed, her beautiful ripe breasts visible.

Joel gazed in awe at their loveliness and sat down, clasped them in both hands, kissed her cleavage, looked deeply into her eyes, and said, "because I don't want to take you."

"I want to be taken."

"That's not what I want." With this, Joel stood up, stepped back several paces, and a sudden foreign fierceness filled his face. "All my life, you have taken from me what you want," and he spat his contempt at her. "Never have you thought of me first."

"Never?"

"Perhaps when you were ten." This time, there was no smile. His anger mounted visibly. "If you think I couldn't have taken you, as you so indelicately put it, you're wrong. You know me even less well than you think you do. Oh, yes, I could have taken you with pleasure, I could have done all sorts of things with you last night when you were too drunk to appreciate what was going on, but I didn't. I gently and tenderly put you to bed, and let you sleep."

"So why hold off now?" she asked sarcastically. "Saint and Martyr, as well as perfect Doctor, are you?"

"I don't believe how cruel you can be, Marcy." His face looked as sad as he felt.

"Don't call me that."

"Why not? It reminds you of what you never let me take, does it?" He glared harshly at her, all thoughts of lovemaking far away, all amorous desire dissipated in the intensity of argument. "You've always called the shots Marcy, always," and he glared again, insisting on using the old endearment. "Well, this time, you'll not get what you want and then dump me."

"What do you want, Joel?"

"The million-dollar question? Work it out for yourself, then come back to me. Go have your shower and come to your senses, you silly, spoilt, rich girl," and with that he was gone.

Marcia lay back on the bed fuming. She was no spoilt rich girl. Work, work, work, had dominated her life. It still did. What sort of a man was this handsome doctor who could have made passionate love to her, she was more than ready and available, and panting with desire for him, as she knew he was for her, but no, he had left her lying there, unsatisfied. Did she know him at all?

Reluctantly, she arose, not bothering to put a bra on, hoping he would see her stomp out to the bathroom, but he was nowhere in sight. She felt a bit uncomfortable putting on Trish's clothes. What sort of man kept his dead wife's clothes? He had handpicked a loose linen top and a medium length, silky, patterned skirt. They matched very well. He had taste. Marcia remembered both garments with some fondness, she even recalled the last time she saw them on Trish. She thought she might have even borrowed the skirt once, it had intricate embroidery and tiny beading around the hem line. Marcia decided to go without any underwear, not wanting to wear the ones she had slept in, and refusing to wear anyone else's.

When she returned, she wandered around the house, in search of Joel, but also curious to see his house. Everything was immaculate, even though she remembered his youth and student accommodation as being a hub of mess, never dirty, cleanliness was crucial to their careers, but shambolic. She admired his taste, the polished wooden floors, the colourful stained-glass windows and doors with Australian wattle and gum leaves featured, the large old urns, with their faded patina and filled with dried, native flowers, the darker heritage colours of the walls, a great feature in contrast to the lighter, very high ceilings. She liked what she saw.

She went in search of the kitchen and noticed that the table was neatly set with a jug of orange juice, a platter of croissants with jams and a pot of coffee. It was all very homely, warm, and inviting. Joel stood, again leaning on the door as was his habit. He wore pale blue, baggy, linen trousers, and a navy, casual, polo top, a man at ease with his body, his looks, his identity. He stepped inside, and they stood opposite ends of the kitchen table, eyes intense, bodies bristling with unspent passion.

"You have a very nice house. I like what you've done with it. It's incredibly different to what I imagined it would be."

"You've changed, I've changed," he said indifferently and shrugged.

They sat down spontaneously, and she served the juice while he poured the coffee. She went to put milk into his coffee, wanting to be helpful, but he grasped her hand. The mere touch of his warmth in her fingers made her feel soft inside.

"Is something wrong?"

"No milk thanks."

"But you always took milk."

"Little things change, as well as the big ones."

They ate a curious breakfast, their eyes never left the other. Joel spilt jam, Marcia dropped her croissant, but neither broke their gaze.

"This is daft, Joel."

"As daft as you want it to be."

"What are we going to do?"

"What are you going to do?"

"What do you want me to do?"

"What do you think you should do?"

This conversation was leading them nowhere and they both saw it. Marcia broke the new silence. "What plans do you have for today?"

"I'm open."

"Yes, but not to me."

"Not open to you. That's a bit rich."

"Let's go to bed. Start all over again. Forget the room I slept in. Let's go to your room instead."

"I'll take you home if you like."

"Home? Didn't you hear me, I said, let's go to bed?"

"I heard you. Didn't you hear me?"

With that question, Marcia stood up and went to his end of the table where she turned furiously at him, and again, started to lash out physically into him, taking her built-up frenzy out onto his body. Almost as if he anticipated it, he grabbed her, pushed her up against the wall, holding his own body away from hers, while she tried to fight him.

"They gave you the right badge at the hospital, didn't they?" Joel snarled at her. "Why do you turn into a raging, angry, scratching, howling pussycat, every time you don't get your way with me?"

After quite a lengthy time, she felt her frenzied energy disappear, and she quivered, and said, "take me home please." Joel put his arm around her and tried to get her to sit down, but she shrugged him off.

"Marcia, you need help badly, you need counsel from a good psychologist. This fury you unleash onto me signals something you have deep inside you that you still have not resolved. Until you do settle it, or come to terms with it, it can never be right within you, or between us."

For once, she didn't argue. She looked bewildered and allowed him to hold her gently in his arms. Leaning her blonde hair on his chest, she felt his warm comfort flow through her. "I don't lose it with anyone else you know. I'm usually so calm and in control."

"I think it's more than control Marcia, I think there is so much repressed anxiety inside you that you don't know what to do with it, so you let it out on me. I'm an obvious target for it. Your cool, icy control disguises this stress."

"I need sex." With that, Joel laughed, helping her to relax a bit more. To his surprise, she launched into questioning him. "Have you had many partners since Trish?"

"Some."

"Is that it?"

"I've not gone without sex Marcia, there have been women, yes, but not since I came back here to Sydney. I have eyes only for you." His eyes were full of love.

Marcia saw the deep warmth, but abruptly asked, "then why didn't you take me?"

"And with that my darling, we have come full circle. If you must keep asking me that, then you are not listening properly to me."

"Take me home Joel, I'm incredibly tired after yesterday, and I shouldn't have drunk so much. I'm sorry. It was nerves. Quite stupid of me. I hope I didn't make a fool of myself. I drunk to ease my panic."

Joel looked sad. "I had hoped that last night would have turned out very differently." He refused to elaborate on his meaning of this, no matter how many times she tried to question him. She was left to wonder whether he would have made love to her if she hadn't drunk so much, or if she hadn't worn such a provocative dress. She'd never know. How silly she was.

16

They drove off silently. Marcia wondered if she would ever get her emotions sorted out, and have a fulfilling private life, or if she was doomed to be a single, career professional.

When Joel drove up her father's drive, she screamed at him. "I don't want to be here."

"Well, I want you to."

"Why?"

"Marcia, you need to get yourself and your emotions sorted, and your father can help you, unless you're willing to let Una help you."

"I couldn't do that, I'd be embarrassed with Una."

"Why? Because she's a nurse and you're a doctor? Does status always have to mean so much to you? She was amazing with me, she was kind, gentle, informative, helpful, patient, encouraging, shall I go on? She is a specialised mental health nurse, as well as a surgical theatre nurse. She's highly trained."

"Yes, no, sometimes."

"You're too status conscious, but that's part of your background."

"And you are a working-class boy makes good."

"If we're going to fight every time we go out, there's no point going out."

"We wouldn't have argued if you hadn't brought me here."

"You mean if you'd got your own way?" With that, Joel got out of the car, opened her door, almost dragged her out, opened the front door with his personal key, gave Bill a cheery hello, and sped off.

All of Marcia's defences rose, and she suspected these two men of plotting on the phone while she had slept. No matter how much Bill tried to coax her to talk about Joel, about Trish, about Una, she would not. When her father dared to mention the name "Rob", she screamed at him for the first time in her life. With that, shame overcame her, she called a taxi and went home. Sad. Alone.

Sleep was what she needed. On Sunday afternoon, she picked up courage and tried to ring Una. If Una could help Joel come to grips with his past and be ready to face the future optimistically, then she should be ready to do that too. No one answered Una's phone, and she was left wondering what to do with herself.

Joel did answer his phone. She decided to take her cue from him. He was pleasant, as he always was, but asked her nothing about her conversation with her father. He did not have too. Marcia knew that Bill would have rung and told him anyway. He made no suggestion to do anything with her, and so, disheartened, she lacked the courage to suggest anything herself.

Over the next days, there were many offers of pre-Christmas drinks after work. Marcia accepted all the invitations, grateful for distractions in the evening, and the excuse to wear some of the new clothes she had splashed out on herself. It did feel good to wear pretty clothes and make-up again. She now looked back almost in horror at photos of herself over the last years in tropical north Australia, the very short hair, plain, unflattering clothes, usually wearing shorts and singlet tops, or very ordinary shift dresses that her elegant, sophisticated mother would have been horrified to see her wearing.

When she went out, she drank two small glasses of wine then switched to sparkling mineral water. Joel was usually in the social group, enjoying the pre-Christmas festivities, but he didn't single Marcia out in any special way at all. Many people spoke directly to her about her startling ball dress, and she found that she was suddenly the focus of attention of many good-looking male nurses, doctors, registrars, and consultants, all who seemed to assume that any woman who wore that sort of dress was clearly unattached, available, and looking for someone special.

She was, but not just anyone. Clearly, Dr Trucker was not paying specific attention to her, so she must be available to them. Joel had known what he was talking about when he expressed reluctance about her wearing such a sexy dress.

Initially, Marcia was shy with the men's advances, but noticing Joel's eyes flash angrily every time a man came too close to her, or touched her affectionately, she perversely took a liking to the novel attention, enjoying this new experience. Indeed, it made her feel younger, lighter in spirit, it brought back memories of the joys of flirting. To the chagrin of all the men, she drew the limit on going home with them, but sometimes, she let their arm drop over her shoulder, all in the excuse of sharing the Christmas cheer. And annoying Joel. Was he jealous? She hoped so.

On Christmas Eve, the social gathering was larger than usual. There was one senior cardiac surgeon that Marcia liked. He made her laugh. On this occasion, she was wearing a strapless pink frock, her hair was loose, and she wore, not her typical red lipstick, but a new, pale pink lipstick. She looked girlish and feminine. She felt young, alive, and ravishing. She was drinking mineral water, wanting to keep her senses alive by not losing control, the night before Christmas. Joel kept an eagle eye on her all night. The surgeon was playing with her hair, letting his hand caress her back and moving his hand closer and closer around her shoulder, slowly sliding it down closer to her bosom. Marcia flicking her hair coquettishly, watched Joel's ire grow.

Una came across to her, and put her arm around Marcia, steering her kindly and deliberately away from this man with explicit desires on her body.

"What are you doing, Dr Knight?"

"Why the formality, Una?"

"Look Marcia, right from the start, I was prepared to be your friend. You've clearly not wanted my friendship. You've treated me as if I was the enemy. Okay, maybe some of the confusion could have been prevented if we had told you right from the start who I was. We thought you'd ask questions. I do look like my twin."

"I can't believe I didn't pick up on that earlier."

"You're still traumatised."

"Yes, perhaps more than I appreciated."

"I've not intervened in any way, although God only knows how much I wanted to. But I will not have you hurt Joel, and that is what you are doing when you blatantly flirt in front of him. Stop it Marcia, come to your senses, and please do it quickly. If you want my help, fine, I heard your messages on my phone, but I wasn't in the right frame of mind then. I've been annoyed at your responses to me and your icy, cool treatment of Joel. But now, I'm willing to talk to you, but you must want my help. Importantly, stop hurting Joel. Outside of Neville, he is my closest male friend, I love him to bits, and hate to see him suffering from so much pain with you playing about in front of him. Imagine if the situation was reversed. How would you feel?"

"And what difference would it mean then?"

"Dr Knight, no offence to you, you're a damn fine doctor, but you've an awful lot of learning to do in the human relationships stakes."

The good-looking surgeon came back on the prowl, in search of his prey, but this time, she would not be caught. The fight had lost its interest and she went out to the car park without a good night to anyone. That was quite churlish, being the night before Christmas.

"Not so fast Marcia," said Joel, waiting, already perched beside her sleek sports car. "What the hell are you playing at?"

"Are you drunk?"

"Perhaps tipsy, give us a lift home, darling," and he fumbled, trying to open the locked door. She opened it and helped him in. My God it was good to have him close to her again.

"I'm a pathetic human, aren't I?"

"Why were you letting that creep maul you?"

"Jealous?"

"Too bloody right," he said, his slurred Australian accent coming out in full.

She snorted her amusement, dropped him off, and went home alone, again, as usual.

Marcia awoke on Christmas morning, thinking how sad it was to wake alone. Her father would be upset that she hadn't gone to the midnight church service with him, but she would see him at breakfast. She dressed in a long, patterned, green dress, a frock with soft fabric, delicate to the touch. Knowing there would be older relatives and people she had not seen for some time, the dress would not scream attention to her body. It was another warm day, and she pulled her hair back casually with a silk green scarf. She liked it long again, the soft curls had returned.

Bundled with her beautifully wrapped presents, she drove to her father's house in contemplative mode. It didn't seem right to be alone on Christmas day, Christmas was about families and children, spontaneous fun, excited shrieks, and novel gifts. That would come later in the day, she knew.

Unsure why she was surprised, she was, when she saw the little old, battered Volkswagen parked at the top of the drive, not in her spot, a little further up. She smiled, glad that Joel was there already. She surmised that he must have gone and got his car early this morning. Exuberantly, he came to the door, no sign of a hangover on his fresh, handsome face. He wore a green linen shirt and bottle green trousers, and they laughed at being unwittingly colour coordinated. Marcia thought quickly that no one would believe they had not planned it. They looked a matching couple. Quirky but quaint.

The three embraced in a group hug and exchanged gifts. Bill always gave books at Christmas, he said it made his life easier. He gave Joel a book on coastal photography and gave Marcia an artistic, pictorial book on the nude body, nudes of all shapes and colours, a very unusual, but pointed gift, from her father. Clearly, he was trying to make a statement.

Joel gave Bill a new golf putter and gave Marcia a gold necklace, with a solid gold dolphin dangling. She knew what this meant, that they had enjoyed so many occasions over their lives shared together in the water, swimming together, like happy frolicking dolphins.

Marcia gave Bill a navy, cashmere jumper, and to Joel, she gave a tiny gold-plated Volkswagen that she had had specially made with his number plates and "save the children" stickers painted on. He knew what this meant, that they had shared many happy times growing up together, racing around in this little car. He loved it as if it was a brand-new car, as slick as her real one, and Bill wisely turned away as Joel took Marcia in his arms and their lips met and stayed joined as if they never wanted to part.

"That's my children," Bill added, "now, let's start the day as it's meant to end, and let these days be long and plentiful," and with that, they ate a plate of delicious tropical fruit, knowing how much food Myra and Sam and their family would shortly arrive with.

The day was full in every sense of the word. Not only did they eat bountiful amounts of delicious, carefully prepared, festive food, but there were so many people that Marcia hadn't seen for years, or who in five years had changed drastically, particularly the children. As she predicted, the younger ones accepted her presence easily as if she had never been away, or more importantly to her, as if nothing traumatic had occurred. Some of the older relatives began to ask more difficult questions she would rather avoid, and every time, Joel seemed to know by the pained expression on her face when it was time to move in and assist her by flattering the older ladies or joking with the older uncles. He was her knight in shining green armour, and today, she felt extreme gratitude to him.

Predictably, they both were the last to hover after having helped to clear up. They sat outside drinking a final bottle of champagne.

"You can't go home my dears, neither of you are in a fair state to drive. You know where the spare bedrooms are."

As doctors, they knew he was right, they'd witnessed too often the desperate plight of road accident victims caused by drunk drivers. Operating on children who had been in a car accident was one of their biggest nightmares, outside of young cancer victims. In his infinite wisdom, Bill kissed his daughter good night, ruffled Joel's hair and went off to bed.

"You've done very well to cope with the crowds today," Joel encouraged her.

"You were a grand help, rescuing me from the clutches of intimate questioning."

"Speaking of intimate questions."

"Let's leave it Joel. It's been a lovely day. Let's keep it like that." She was surprising herself.

They walked down to the garden and sat in the rocking swing, comfortable with the closeness of each other's body, not wanting to spoil anything by talking and ending the day possibly arguing. They dare not touch for fear of losing control in the forbidden garden of their childhood and youthful games. They had spent countless nights together on this swing, chatting about the meaning of life.

After a long time, Joel lifted Marcia's face to the moon, looked tenderly at her, and said, "I can't keep it from you any longer Marcia, and Christmas day is a wonderful day to say this -- I love you."

"You love me?" Utter amazement filled her face.

"Yes Marcia, I love you," and he kissed her gently, but with deep passion on her lips. She did not respond fully, her senses aroused, but feeling a little tipsy from the drink, she was not absorbing his claim totally yet, and she wanted to soak its meaning fully.

"You love me?" Marcia asked again and shaking her head as if this was not what she fully believed, she rose, tottering on her feet.

"Go in my love, I'll lock-up," and with that, Marcia ambled slowly off to her old bedroom, leaving Joel fully in command.

17

Christmas night! Marcia lay in bed in a blissful waiting state. Joel, this wonderful charismatic man who had been part of her life, all her life, except for these last five years, really did love her. How amazing! What a Christmas present! It was the very best!

Why had he taken so long to declare his love for her? Importantly, why had he married Trish first? In her heart of hearts, she knew the correct answer to this, and the knowledge of her personal responsibility made her squirm uncomfortably. What sort of an idiot was she? She was by no means an innocent observer in his love life or lack of it. She had been silly, incredibly stupid. It was time to make amends.

Her parents' house was enormous, the master bedroom was quite a distance from Marcia's old bedroom. There had always been enough privacy as she was growing up. As a teenager, it was like she had her own wing in the house. Assuming Joel would come into her old room as he had done countless times before, she threw off the light cover and looked down at her slim, naked body. Yes, it was in as good a shape as it ever had been, tightly toned and bristling with anticipation.

"That's some gorgeous body, Marcia," said a deep, quiet, masculine voice from the doorway.

"Come in Joel," replied Marcia, turning toward the voice, and sitting up to lean on one elbow, her full bosoms turning toward him. "You look gorgeous, sexy and intriguing." He held his ground from a distance. She read his desire, and knowing her own, slid one hand seductively down her thigh, letting it pause near her hidden parts, parts screaming to be explored. The mere sight of him standing watching her made her wet with longing.

"You're gorgeous."

"Come in Joel," she begged, sitting up and holding her arms out to him.

Instead of rushing in to grasp the woman who had preoccupied his attention for most of his life, he stepped gingerly and slowly into the room. It was such a familiar room. Her parents had left it intact when she went to university, and when her mother had died, her father wanted to keep it as it was, even more so, as a memorial of memories, remembering the countless times his dear wife had gone in to talk and laugh with their daughter.

Joel stood soaking in Marcia's beauty and sexiness with lustful intensity evident in his brown eyes. Every second he met her gaze whetted her appetite, but he was deliberately stretching the time. This was a moment to be savoured, not a moment to be rushed.

Marcia watched his back muscles tighten as he went to shut the door, slowly, symbolically, shutting them together in the same room of longing. She could almost smell the sex in the air, it hovered, unspoken, yet present in its rich, full anticipation.

Joel slowly unbuttoned his shirt and placed it carefully over a chair. This was not the Joel she remembered, who in his youth, would throw his clothes off with carefree abandon. This was a mature man, a man who had witnessed complex layers of life, and knew what he wanted from it, and from his woman.

How could his emotions be so controlled? Marcia had thrown her clothes off in a hapless pile. She felt wanton, a woman ready to lose constraint in a sexual frenzy. Frustrated by his slow build-up, she leapt out of bed, and threw her arms around Joel's enormous, expansive, well-toned chest to grasp his tight, muscular, swimmer's back. Her hands reached up to his hair, feeling his thick curls, then raced down to his trousers, fumbling to loosen the belt that he had already loosened, and reaching for his fly that he had already unzipped. Joel expertly stepped out of his trousers and loafers, and with haste, threw off his underpants.

For a split second, they stepped back in amazement, the realisation of both being fully naked reviving painful memories, the pain dissipated in the ecstasy of the moment. As quickly as their bodies moved away, they drew together as magnets, unable if they tried to be ripped apart. Their attraction compelled union, the force of nature was at work, nothing could stand in the way, they were meant for each other.

Destiny! Doctor Ice Maiden had melted in a pool of hot desire.

Their hands roamed freely over each other's bodies, nowhere was out of bounds. The bodies felt familiar, yet strange, known, yet curiously novel. Excitement mounted with these contradictions, face-to-face, cheek to cheek, different but desired, touched yet still to be touched.

Their lips locked in a kiss that seemed timeless. Every part of their lips was to be rediscovered and explored. Joel was an expert kisser and took Marcia's breath away. Did this man kiss for a living? Did his life depend on technique and feeling? He was a master in his trade.

Was Marcia so severely out of practice? However, there was no restraint in her now, her breath was quicker, and she gasped out aloud, every time he tried something new. They mutually increased and decreased the pressure of their lips, frantic to arouse and be aroused. Joel nibbled her lower lip, daring to bite her gently as he heard her ecstatic gasps of delight, and heard her suck in her breath in amazement at his power to stimulate her senses to the full. She was alive, every sense alert to stimulation.

Joel placed his arms around Marcia and picked her up. It was so beautiful to be cradled in his arms, she was teary with delight, and she leaned back on his muscular chest for a moment, almost child-like. Marcia wanted far more than comfort, she wanted sex like she had never wanted it, or perhaps this frantic desire was what passion was like many years ago. She squirmed in his arms until he moved over to the bed and dropped her lightly down. For a few seconds, he stood over her, high on the bed, his manly features throbbing. What a sight! Marcia could not restrain herself, she clasped at his legs, pulling him down, and he crashed down clumsily onto her.

The bodies writhed in a tangled twirl, and they giggled in delight. Joel constantly moved into different positions. Marcia, whimpering in desire, kept reaching for Joel's fuller action.

"Joel, why do you keep holding back from me?" Marcia cried out, her head thrashing wildly from side to side, the desire making her feel totally, utterly, and wonderfully out of control, a novel experience for her. "I want you Joel, I want every part of you, I want you inside me. Come into me."

With that, Joel's tongue darted into her warm, wet depths, tasting its arousal, arousing her further. His tongue delved deeply and came out to lick her further. He knew precisely how to combine his kisses, wet licks, and sucking, as he listened to her urgent breathing and writhing motions. When he nibbled her, biting gently into the depths of her desire, Marcia gave the scream of contented ecstasy he had longed to hear, and she had longed to utter. In his imagination, he had heard the cry, contented, satiated, fulfilled, satisfied, unique to her loveliness. How often the idea of it had satisfied his lonely nights.

"My darling, to hear you cry out like that is heaven to my ears. Marcy baby, I love you, I love you, I love you." Joel moved to kiss her lips again, mixing tastes and then swooped down to her breasts. "Keep coming and coming and coming. I want to hear you scream all day, my lovely one."

"Joel, I want you, come inside me," Marcia begged. "I want to satisfy you. I want to feel you inside me."

Joel's response was to grab the heavy cotton sheet and throw it over her body. "I can't darling," and Joel lay his body over hers and nestled into her breasts. Gently at first, he fondled one and then the other, then rubbed his hands roughly over her nipples making them leap to attention. Swooping on to their height, he sucked gently, then harder, sucking as though his life depended on it. Her murmurs of delight were music to his ears.

However, no matter how satisfied she felt so far, her entire body shrieked with desire to be totally and fully at one with this man.

"Joel, throw off this ridiculous sheet, come inside me, now."

"Not now, darling."

"Joel, what are you playing at? If I don't have you inside me, I'll burst, I will go crazy. You're gorgeous and I want you fully."

Nothing prepared Marcia for Joel's response. He got up and walked away as if he had no more business with her.

Her voice was desperate. "Joel, come back, I need you, don't leave me. Where are you going?" Marcia's body was glistening with sweat and sexual energy, she felt abundantly alive. Nothing could break this energy flow except for the departure of the wonderful man who was igniting her. "Joel, please don't leave," and she raced out of bed to grasp whatever part of his body she could. She latched onto his firm buttocks and held them tightly.

"Sh, my darling, I'm just going away to get a towel."

"A towel?" Marcia shook her head in disbelief. "Have you lost your senses?"

"No, not quite, although I'd like to, but I don't want you to lose yours."

"I want to. I want to lose myself entirely in you."

"You can't."

"I don't understand what's going on. You send out signals that you want me. You incite me to a frenzy of desire, then just as I've never wanted you so much, you leave me in search of something as boring as a towel." Marcia grabbed his ankles and would not let him go. Now, she was crying. "I want you Joel, I want you, I need you. I've not been with a man for more than five years. Don't leave me, I need you."

"Me Marcy? Or any man?"

"Don't say that Joel, you're not just any man."

"No, but would any man do?"

"No, you're quite unique and you know it."

"Yes, and?" Joel paused to let his eyes roamed lustfully over her lascivious body. He persisted, "unique and what?"

"And what? Stop taunting me. Make love with me Joel."

"And is it making love Marcia, or is it having sex, something you've been deprived of for more than five years?"

"Joel, why are you complicating things?" Marcia felt overwhelmed. The tiredness of the last few days suddenly crashed in on her and she flopped on the rug beside the bed and curled up on Joel's lap. Joel stroked her back and lay his head down on her blond head. In a short time, she'd fallen asleep. It had been an emotional day, mixing with relatives and Joel's extended family, and everything had caught up with her, seeing people she had not seen since the traumas of the past, and they both had consumed a fair amount of festive drink.

Joel stroked Marcia until he could hear her breathing deeply. Gently, he picked her up and lay her back on the bed on her side. The thought that they were so close, yet still, so far away from each other, grieved him sorely. He pulled the cover over this beautiful woman's slender body. He ran his fingers gently over her narrow waist, under her breasts, and under her full lips. Responding to the touch in her sleep, she reached out to touch his body, and murmured, "Rob? Rob, come to me, make love to me."

Joel had no answer to this. Lust vanished in an instant, and with it, the love he had felt. His usual calm demeanour changed, as furious anger filled his entire countenance. Rob? Is that who she thinks of in her dreams? Rob? Is this the man who still fills this woman's fantasies? Joel could hardly take it in. Rob, the man who had stood in between his love and dreams, who had wreaked havoc on his hopes for eternal love.

What an ending to Christmas Day!

18

In fury, Joel snatched his clothes and went into the guest room that unbeknown to Marcia, had lately become like his own spare room. Often after a hard day's work, he called around uninvited, but always welcome, to chat with the old man who loved and nurtured him as his own son. After more than one bottle of fine wine, he was grateful of the offer to stay overnight, and even kept some basic clothes and toiletries here now. Marcia was so out of touch with the daily patterns of her father's life, that she hadn't even guessed how much time Joel spent with her father.

Marcia slept long into Boxing Day and woke abruptly, having an uncomfortable sensation of being watched. She was. Joel sat in a chair by the window, the morning's rays catching his dark hair. He looked handsome and refined. Somewhat mature. A man sure of himself. She remembered the night of half fulfilment and her desire mounted. Something in her detected his cold restraint. While she sat up, breasts exposed and pushed her hair back from her face, she smiled, and held out her arms, expecting Joel to fall into them. He didn't.

"Good morning," he said curtly.

"What's wrong?" Marcia asked, and instinctively went to cover her body. An enormous cloud covered Joel's face. He was unusually dark. There was not a glimmer of light, no typical flicker of amusement on the face, no appealing caresses in his eyes. He sat staring. She felt fully exposed, like he was an x-ray machine penetrating her innermost being, and she did not like it one little bit. What she hid in her depths was for no one's eyes.

"Sleep well?" Joel asked in a matter-of-fact tone.

"Well enough. Joel, why are you being so uptight with me, what have I done wrong? Is dad okay?"

"Oh yes, Bill, with his usual, thoughtful foresight, has left a note saying that he's gone to your Auntie Agnes's place for Boxing Day. I'm sure his intention was to leave us to have the sort of day I had dreamed of having, the house to ourselves, the pool to frolic in, empty bedrooms to roam and romp through."

Joel's face was so dark that Marcia did not go over and smooth his worried brow, but she had to discover what was wrong. "So why can't we have that sort of day?" Her attempt to sound light-hearted failed.

"After last night? Are you kidding?"

"But I thought we were having such a lovely time last night. The only problem I remember was you getting up to get something ridiculous like a towel."

"That's right, when the going gets rough, blame me."

"Blame you? Joel, what are you on about?" Marcia wondered if it was safe to move closer to him, but he sat rigidly in the chair, a grim resolve on his chin, no warm inviting look on his face at all, so she did not approach him.

"Marcia, go and have a shower and get some clothes on, and then we need to talk."

"I don't want to talk, I want to make love."

"You wouldn't know what that meant."

"Are you casting aspersions on my lovemaking?" Hurt and

bewilderment cast a shadow over her face. Joel looked away, the combination gave her an alluring appeal she didn't often display, and his masculine ego could not afford to be tempted.

"What would I know about your lovemaking?" He asked gruffly, and with an aloofness he only partly felt. Today, it was anger that predominated his emotions.

Defying Joel's fury, Marcia arose naked and stood before him, close but not touching. Quietly, with sadness in her voice, Marcia asked, "if it wasn't lovemaking, we were doing last night, what were we doing?"

"You tell me."

"I was making love."

"So, do you love me?" Joel put his head right up against her head, but the look in his eyes frightened her. "You can't make love to someone you don't love, or you are just having sex, and that's not the same thing." He spat the words out, angrily, slowly, so that every word sank in.

"Don't look at me like that. You're frightening me, Joel."

"You've never stop frightening me, Marcy."

"I don't understand where this is going."

"Neither do I."

Silence hovered, an uncomfortable heavy silence. Joel continued to sit still, anger conspicuous on his face, his body rigid, unyielding. Marcia suddenly felt uptight with her nakedness but didn't want to display her unease. Anyway, Joel wasn't looking at her body at all, his deep brown eyes fixed only and steadfastly on her radiant blue eyes, crippling her confidence, and she moved away, and sat back coyly on the bed, pulling the crumpled sheet back over her, covering her body.

"Joel, what have I done to make you so furious with me?"

"Work it out yourself." His hostility was palpable.

"I can't."

"Unless you sit down properly with me and talk and talk and talk until there is no more talk needed between us, this sort of thing is going to happen all the time."

"What sort of thing?"

Joel gave her a glare. "You're not stupid woman, work it out," and he rose haughtily and left the room.

Marcia raced after him, grabbing him by the shirt sleeve, but he gave her such a withering grimace that she walked away, upset, in incredulous disbelief at the change of events.

Being surrounded by water had often consoled her as a child, and she went and put on her old maiden aunt swimsuit as she called it, fit to be seen only when maiden aunts called. She dived in and swam length after length until the tears came crashing out and she hurled herself out of the pool, and threw herself onto an outside armchair, dripping wet, tears hurtling down her face.

Joel stared, even now, his face was not melting with the sight of her tears. Anger still dominated his features, a rage she had rarely seen, all these years of knowing him with the closeness with which she did.

It took some time to calm herself, she felt alone in the universe. Yet she sat here with the man who only last night had declared his love for her, whom she thought was going to make wild, passionate love, who had started to, then went off in pursuit of, now what was it again? Yes, a towel.

"Why the hell did you go off last night for a towel?"

"Because naive Doctor woman, I had no condoms on me. Contrary to your ridiculous ideas about me, I'm no longer in the practice of sleeping with women or needing to carry something, just in case I get lucky. Furthermore, I presume that after these years of celibacy, you're not on any form of contraception."

"Last night, I didn't care about contraception. I only cared about you."

"Yes, I know that, but next month, you might have cared about the consequences."

"I don't believe you went in pursuit of a towel, what were you going to do with it? Stuff it up me?" Her attempt at weak humour was lost.

"Hardly, I was just going to lay it between us as some form of barrier. Child-like, teenage tactics."

"Hardly full-proof."

"I agree, but better than nothing. Back to teenage practices."

Again, they sat in mutual madness, both glaring stubbornly at each other. Marcia broke the insane silence. "Dad didn't give us this day free together here for nothing. Can't we enjoy it?"

"No." Today, Joel was calling all the shots, he refused to be trifled with. His masculine ego was dented, and he was not going to give in to this woman's whim, no matter how adorable she looked, even in the ridiculously outdated bathing costume.

"Aren't you being daft? Your bluntness is a bit harsh, isn't it?"

"You're a bit harsh."

"Joel," she pleaded, coming over to stroke his back. Her touch didn't even come close to him. Joel lashed out aggressively and pushed her arm away.

Coolly, he replied, "Marcia, go and have a shower, get properly dressed, cover yourself up, you have clothes from the past in your wardrobe, and come and make coffee, then we will talk. You are to talk fully to me. Put all your cards on the table. All of them, do you understand? There's to be no more messing around with my head, or my heart." Could anyone defy his authority? "Tell me about these last five years and talk through all the issues you keep avoiding mentioning. I'll accept nothing less than the full story."

Marcia hated anyone telling her what to do. She was the stubborn and willful one, not him, she couldn't cope with Joel trespassing on her emotional territory. "Don't tell me what to do." Her words were cruel, they were meant to hurt. They did. The gap between them was growing bigger with every second. Marcia could hardly believe they had ever been intimate last night, she could hardly believe that she thought they were going to make love. She thought they were making love. Something must've happened, and she racked her brain to try to think what it might be. She couldn't work it out.

"Go and change Marcia, put clothes on to make yourself decent, nothing provocative. Convince me, rather than seduce me, persuade me, rather than prance in front of me." This was the voice of authority, demanding, intimidating, unnerving. He was the lion, the King of the Jungle. She was a quivering pussy cat. It was strange and foreign and frightening, and she hated it.

Again, Marcia broke down and howled, big tears of what she wasn't sure, that they were real were painfully obvious, and yet Joel watched, unmoved. "What did I do wrong Joel? What's made you so angry?"

Joel stood up and came and stood over her, his height hovering menacingly. His face held a serious sadness that she was totally unaccustomed to seeing. With venom in his tone, he spat out the reply. "I thought we were making love too, Marcia," and he paused to glare at her and through her. "But you fell asleep on the floor. That was okay. I was worried about neither of us having contraception, and we'd had a lovely time anyway. I picked you up and lifted you back into bed. When I went to kiss you goodnight, you called out for Rob."

"Rob?" Surprised horror filled Marcia's face.

"Yes, Rob." Every ounce of emotion he had ever felt toward Rob could be heard in his answer, and Marcia shivered as if she was freezing cold.

"Rob? You're just saying that, you're just making things up to complicate things."

"How very wrong you are, my love."

"My love? That seems a joke, now, doesn't it?"

Ignoring her, Joel continued. "If you have any idea how I'm sick of my life being complicated by you, you wouldn't say that. But last night, when you uttered that word 'Rob', that was it. I am bloody well sick and tired of your ridiculous evasiveness, pretending that nothing major has ever happened between us, then when I come close to broaching the past, you turn into a ridiculous child and attack me like some wild, feral cat, then when I tell you I love you, you call out not for me, but for Rob."

"I didn't call out for Rob."

"Marcy, you did. Now go inside, get showered, dress in plain clothes, make us a pot of strong coffee, and come back and talk to me. And I mean talk properly, everything, get it out of your system once and for all, no messing around. Everything Marcia, I mean it, get it all out," and with that, Joel started to scream at her. Years of pent-up frustration of waiting in vain had escalated way beyond his ability to cope, and his screams revealed all. "Get it out. Everything. Every damn last bit of repression that's holding you back, and not letting us develop the sort of mature relationship we would have developed years ago, if you hadn't been the stupid, stubborn, selfish person you are. Get it out, out, out. Do you hear me woman? Get it all out."

His voice reverberated through the backyard, and she shivered in fear and ran inside, unusually compliant. Pussycat submits to lion!

19

Marcia showered and dressed in plain denim shorts and a white cotton tee-shirt and went into the kitchen. She noticed how much cleaning had been done in the kitchen and assumed that Joel had got up early to do so. He was such a good man. She brewed strong coffee and cut some Christmas cake, remembering how this used to be one of Joel's favourite cakes. She wondered if it still was, and who had baked the cake.

Suddenly, as if in a revelation, she realised that she didn't really know this man anymore. She no longer knew his everyday likes and dislikes, his goals, and fears. Five years was a long time in anyone's life to be absent.

It was a beautiful sunny day, but for an Australian Boxing Day, the heat was not overpowering. The overhead fans in the patio kept a gentle breeze flowing and wafted the fragrance of the overhanging tropical plants. Bill kept a neat and pretty garden flourishing. Marcia placed the coffee, cake, and a jug of iced water gingerly down on the table.

Trying to begin with a light-hearted tone, Marcia began, "is Christmas cake still one of your favourites?"

"Yes, but I always preferred your mother's cakes to my mother's. Your mum could afford fine brandy to moisten her cakes with, my mum couldn't. She used orange juice. This is my mother's cake, she made one for your father. She has every year since your mother died."

"She's so kind. It's tasty." These reminders of the differences in their upbringing kept cropping up. They sat, uncomfortable with their grumpiness, gazing at the pretty garden.

Joel made the first move. "Okay Marcia, I'll begin. I'll start as I hope you mean to, with utmost honesty."

"Of course."

Doubting that, he began. "I have a confession to make."

"Oh." She looked startled, wondering what was to follow.

"I had a few scouts up in Darwin who fed me information about you."

"What? You had spies? Who?"

"They were hardly spies. I keep a wide circle of friends open Marcia, these scouts were medical acquaintances of mine who I was asking a few simple questions. They worked with you or knew of your fine work."

"Who?"

"You don't need to know that. I simply wanted to know that you were alive and well, and not being self-destructive."

"Why would I have been?"

"Because you left us so abruptly, and in such a fierce rage."

"With good reason."

"I had good reason too, remember that, but I didn't leave everyone worrying about my absence and the state of my mental health."

Silence reigned. Joel poured chilled water into two tall glasses and then went inside to fill up the jug.

"What did they say, these spies of yours?"

"That you are an excellent doctor, that you did a lot of good work in the community, that you did more general practice than anaesthesia, but you excelled in whatever medical work you did. Oh yes, and that the Aboriginal kids adored you."

"What else?"

"That you were quiet, you kept to yourself, you rarely socialised, even at the weekends, and didn't seem to have a boyfriend."

"Would it have mattered if I did?"

"Of course, it would have. But they said you hardly had a girl-friend, let alone a boyfriend."

"How would they know?"

"They said Darwin has a small town feel and everyone knows everyone."

"That's true."

"Did you know anything about my life?"

"Not really." Marcia looked away embarrassed. "I can't believe myself. Of course, I should have known that you would have come back to Sydney, back to dad's old hospital. I should have realised that. Over the years, he's told us countless stories about his old job. He must be abundantly proud of you having his esteemed position." She looked far away into the middle distance, a thousand thoughts flooding through her.

Joel nodded but looked very sad. "Didn't your father ever mention me?"

She was evasive. "I've been a rotten daughter. I've been a terrible friend. I didn't ask him questions about anyone, including you. I've not been a good daughter at all. I contacted him on his birthday, Father's Day, and Christmas, that's about it. I didn't even visit him for five years. I admit it, I've been pathetic, totally caught up in dealing with my own screwed-up emotions, and not doing a very good job of it."

Joel's face softened with her admission of guilt. "Marcia, would you please begin at the start of the story, go back to our university days, and tell me why you went for Rob."

"Do we have to do this?"

"Yes, we do." His face was determined. He was not for budging.

"I was always jealous of you."

"What?" This was not what Joel was expecting to hear. "Jealous of me? You, who had every material possession a young woman could want? You, who are beautiful and clever, with parents who adored you? You, who had life on a plate, a silver spoon hanging from your mouth the day you were born? Jealous of me, who has had to struggle every minute of my life?"

"I imagine you're hardly struggling now."

"Keep to the point." His tone was gruff. "Why were you jealous of me then?"

"With your personality, life seemed easy, everyone loved you."

"Everyone loves you too, you just don't seem to see it, or appreciate it."

An awkward gap in the conversation hovered. Marcia began again, tentatively, brushing her hair away from her face with nervous gestures that were not typical. "It really began with University. We both won scholarships to Melbourne, back then, we thought we were so clever."

"I didn't assume any cleverness, for me it was simply hard work. I'd earned the scholarship. I was grateful for the scholarship. It meant that I could go to medical school and not have to rely entirely on your father's handouts, even though he kept sending me gifts."

"I think it was in our third year when we both joined the University drama society."

"Yes, it was." Joel knew that talk of the drama society was to herald the start of a discussion about their respective previous partners. It had been such a long time since their names had been mentioned together. The time had come to do so.

"Trish came in as head of the drama club and I knew you'd fallen for her instantly." She waved a hand, not letting him interrupt.

"Why wouldn't you? She was a fiery red-headed beauty, everyone fell in love with her. She could mimic any accent, have you laughing or crying, whatever she wanted. She was such an accomplished actress, her presence on stage was sensational."

"It was." Joel still looked sad as a thousand and one memories flooded back. "Go on."

"I was so jealous."

"How was I to know that?"

"I thought it was obvious."

"It wasn't. Sometimes you're as closed as a book. As icy as an icicle. As hard as an iceberg. As cold as a freezer. An Ice Maiden."

She tried to ignore his insults. "When Rob joined the drama society too, I thought it would be a bit of fun to flirt with him, while you were flirting with Trish."

"My God Marcia, initially, I wasn't flirting with Trish. I just enjoyed her company and admired her skills as a brilliant actress. Rob was the jealous one. He was always frustrated that either you or I topped every medical exam. He couldn't cope with that, he wanted to be top dog. Trying to get you was his way of dethroning me. Didn't you see that?"

"I thought you'd drop Trish if I started going out with Rob."

"But we were never going out. From the day we left home, you and I agreed to remain the best friends we have always been, until we finished medical school. We made a pact, sitting here, around the pool, before we left for Melbourne."

"Well, that was naive, wasn't it?"

"No, I thought it was a sensible understanding, and something we agreed to keep."

"You fell for Trish."

"She was warm to me Marcia, quite gentle and loving. Your iciness has frozen me out time and time again. The moment Rob got his hands onto you, you began to cut yourself off from me."

"What a mess!" Marcia got up and walked down to the swing, the old favourite place she went to in many a troubled time, letting her pain go back and forward, before final release.

Joel stayed where he was, then went into the kitchen to make lunch. He brought a colourful salad out, and wordlessly, Marcia joined him. For a while, they ate in silence, neither knowing how to begin.

"Marriage Marcia, why on earth did you marry Rob Collins?"

"Marriage Joel, why on earth did you marry Trish Byrne?"

In a barely audible voice, she whispered, "because I seemed to have lost you."

"Oh my God, Marcia! You have never lost me, not for a single minute of any day. Why didn't you talk to me?"

"I don't know. It seems stupid now. But that's why we escaped and had a small registry office wedding. I knew that dad had always expected me to have the full, white, church wedding marrying you and I couldn't face him. It was pathetic of me, I didn't even invite him to the wedding, I didn't invite any family, I just told them after the formalities had taken place."

"I always wondered why."

"And why did you sneak off and do the same?"

"Same answers as you. I couldn't face my family's disappointment that I wasn't marrying you, and as for your father, I knew the hurt he'd feel. Don't get me wrong. When you were married, it was like you did it to spite me. That's how I saw it, but I tried to come to some acceptance of our positions. I then grew to love Trish very much." He looked away. "But I never stopped loving you, never ever. You were always there present in our relationship, the unspoken third person. Trish knew it, but she was decent enough to not bring it up. But she saw the way I still looked at you with such burning desire, I saw the recognition in her eyes." He looked away again. "Every day that I woke and looked at Trish, I wondered why it wasn't you in the bed beside me. She comprehended what my look was about. She deserved far more than that. She was a good woman, very like her twin sister."

Marcia wandered back to the swing. After quite some time, Joel walked over to sit on the second swing and asked the million-dollar question. "That fateful day, why did you suggest what you did?" Marcia swayed quietly, refusing to answer, just shaking her head vehemently. "Marcia, please answer me. You must talk to me about everything before we have any chance of moving on."

"I knew I'd made a stupid, big mistake in marrying Rob. Whereas you grew to love Trish, I didn't ever love Rob as a wife should love her husband. My jokey suggestion on that night was my way of trying to deal with my blunder in a light-hearted fashion, to cover my feelings and give you a bit of a hint."

"So, when we all came back to Sydney for that brief holiday, and went out for dinner together, and you suggested we swap partners to drive back to the hotel, did you really think we were going to sleep in the same bed that night?"

"I've deliberately made sure that that night is a blur to me."

"Well, it's clear to me. Rob and I shouldn't have been driving our hire cars."

"Yes, and I should have been with Rob. That way I'd be dead, and Trish would be with you."

They remained silent. Too many shocking memories were racing around their minds. Joel got off the swing and took Marcia by the hand and led her back to the table.

"Now, I have to look at you directly in the eyes. Marcia, the accident was a tragedy, as all car accidents are. Rob couldn't have anticipated the car that swerved into his car, smashing the restaurant window. The accident had nothing to do with us having had one drink too many, stupid medical students who should have known better, having a night out on the town. The coroner ruled that it was the other car's fault, one hundred percent."

"I know, but I should have been in that car with my husband. I should be dead. You should have your wife alive and beside you now."

"None of us knows why tragic things like this happen, Marcia. Grief hits us differently. I was blessed by having amazing support from all my family, as well as from your father." This did not go unnoticed.

"Dear old dad."

"Yes, your dad and my family helped me to see all the good things that were remaining in my life, and they kept me sane. This didn't mean that I didn't feel the extreme loss, of course I did. Trish was a lovely woman, we had precious times together. Even though I felt that she knew I loved you the most, she never talked about it, and never let that cause a rift between us. She even knew when to walk away and give me space when she saw what she called 'that look' come into my eyes."

"That's quite incredible. I couldn't be that gracious."

"And don't get me wrong, I did love her, but I grew to love her. I should not have married her in the first place. All my life, I have loved you, Marcy. Believe me. You are my first love. I always thought that when the time was right, I would tell you this, and we would marry, and begin our own family. But we agreed that we wouldn't talk about it until we finished medical school. You broke our agreement."

"I am truly sorry, Joel." Remorse could be heard in her voice.

Joel wanted to finish his story. "Una coming into my life was an amazing step in my journey from loss to rediscovering life. She is such a good woman."

"Were you tempted to marry her?"

162 - LARISSA LOVEJOY

"Oh Marcia, please listen to me. I have just said that I have always loved you. You. Are you listening to me? Please do, I have always loved you, that's right, you. I'll keep repeating myself. I have always loved you. Una is a darling, I adore her as my sister-in-law. She played a massive role in my recovery. She helped me to heal. When you disappeared after the funerals, my world fell apart. Mum, dad, Bill, and eventually Una, kept me afloat." He watched her taking it all in. It was a lot to absorb. "And you Marcia, did you love Rob, and why did you disappear?"

Marcia sat very still, not looking at Joel for a long time. He was a patient man. Eventually she began. "Only sort of," she grimaced.

Relieved, Joel grinned, "only sort of?"

"Yes, the marriage was a crazy spur of the moment. It was a thoroughly, stupid response. Madly irresponsible. I was trying to hurt you, I realise that now. I was jealous of how much dad was devoted to you."

"Oh Marcia, that's just ridiculous, he nurtured me as a future son-in-law, because of his love for you."

"I know." At last, they smiled amicably with each other.

"Fancy a glass of white wine? It is Boxing Day." She smiled and nodded.

Joel came back with an ice bucket and a bottle of chilled Clare Valley Riesling, a box of praline chocolates on the side.

"I should go on while I've got the courage to do so."

"Yes, my love, you should."

"I totally blamed myself for the accident, and couldn't cope seeing you, which is why I went to the Northern Territory."

"Did you have to go so far away?" He looked at her intently. "And did you have to stay away for so long?"

"Yes. Perhaps I regret staying away for as long as I did, and I acknowledge I've not been a good daughter. Dad needed me more after he lost mum, and he lost a daughter as well."

"I've been here for him."

"You're a very good man." This time, there was no sarcasm in her tone. She had melted the icicles that had bound her softness. Her love could flow out at last.

"Marcia, you have to accept that you were not the cause of the accident that led to our spouses' deaths."

"I'm nearly there."

"Oh, my darling."

"I think working with the Aboriginal kids helped me to redeem my conscience, not that the tragedy was anything to do with them of course, I just felt like I was giving a lot to the community, and I was helping others make a better life."

"Yes, that's exactly what my spies said." He grinned warmly at her, and poured a glass of crisp, dry wine.

They sat in comfortable silence. Marcia broke it. She moved her seat closer and took Joel's hand in hers. Quietly, she said, "Joel, I've been rotten to you, too many times. For this, I am sorry, deeply sorry."

"You're forgiven." He meant it.

"I love you, Joel, I always have too."

At this, Joel's eyes brimmed with tears. "Do you mean it, Marcy?"

"Yes, and every time you call me that, it's been a prompt, a reminder of your love for me, and my love for you. I've just been ridiculously stubborn in admitting it. Like you, I have always known that you are my first and only true love."

With this, Joel pulled her onto his lap and kissed her, long and gently. "Dr Marcia Knight, nee Collins, previously my childhood, sandpit girlfriend, Marcia Newton, I love you, will you marry me?"

"Dr Joel Trucker, always Joel Trucker, I love you, and yes, I will marry you, at long last."

"Well, well, this sounds like it calls for a celebration." Joel had seen Bill appear quietly in the background, and had proceeded with his proposal, wanting to have this dear old man who had been like a father to him, finally hear what he had longed to hear all his life.

"I'm a bit old-fashioned, I guess I should ask you Bill for your daughter's hand in marriage."

Marcia swung around to see her father amble across to them. Bill joined the pair of young hands in his old, slightly arthritic hands. He kissed his daughter on the top of her head and slapped Joel on the back. "I have my chosen son-in-law at last! Yes, I give you my blessing, if I can walk down the aisle with my darling daughter. Now, there's a bottle of Krug champagne tucked away exactly for an occasion just like this, I'll put the lid on your white wine, and go and get it."

"Destiny darling, we were meant for each other," and Joel tucked Marcia into his side as if he was never going to let her go.

At last, love had melted the ice.